Hold the Dark

HOLD THE DARK

A Novel

WILLIAM GIRALDI

LIVERIGHT PUBLISHING CORPORATION
A DIVISION OF W. W. NORTON & COMPANY
NEW YORK   LONDON

For information about permission to reproduce selections from this book,
write to Permissions, Liveright Publishing Corporation,
a division of W. W. Norton & Company, Inc.,
500 Fifth Avenue, New York, NY 10110

For information about special discounts for bulk purchases, please contact
W. W. Norton Special Sales at specialsales@wwnorton.com or 800-233-4830

Manufacturing by RR Donnelley Harrisonburg
Book design by Daniel Lagin
Production manager: Julia Druskin

Library of Congress Cataloging-in-Publication Data

Giraldi, William.
  Hold the dark : a novel / William Giraldi. — First edition.
    pages cm
  ISBN 978-0-87140-667-5 (hardcover)
  1. Wilderness areas—Alaska—Fiction. 2. Wolves—Fiction. 3. Families—
Alaska—Fiction. 4. Revenge—Fiction. 5. Missing persons—Fiction.
  6. Alaska—Fiction. 7. Suspense fiction. I. Title.
  PS3607.I469H65 2014
  813'.6—dc23
                                    2014023730

Liveright Publishing Corporation
500 Fifth Avenue, New York, N.Y. 10110
www.wwnorton.com

W. W. Norton & Company Ltd.
Castle House, 75/76 Wells Street, London W1T 3QT

1 2 3 4 5 6 7 8 9 0

For Aiden Xavier, may your dark always be on hold.

O unteachably after evil, but uttering truth.

—Gerard Manley Hopkins

We fear the cold and the things we do not understand. But most of all we fear the doings of the heedless ones among ourselves.

—Eskimo shaman to explorer Knud Rasmussen

Hold the Dark

I

The wolves came down from the hills and took the children of Keelut. First one child was stolen as he tugged his sled at the rim of the village, another the following week as she skirted the cabins near the ice-choked pond. Now, in the rolling snow whorls of the new winter, a third was dragged from their village, this one from his own doorstep. Noiseless—not a scream, not a howl to give witness.

The women were frantic, those who had lost their children inconsolable. Police arrived from town one afternoon. They scratched sentences into notepads. They looked helpful but never returned to the village. Both women and men patrolled the hills and borders with rifles. Even the elderly, armed with pistols, escorted children home from the schoolhouse and church. But no one would send a party past the valleys to hunt the wolves.

The six-year-old son of Medora Slone was the third to be taken. She told her fellow villagers how she had trekked over the hills and across the vale all that evening and night and into the blush of dawn with the rifle across her back and a ten-inch knife strapped to her thigh. The revenge she wanted tasted metallic. The tracks of the wolves became scattered and vague, then vanished in the flakes falling like feathers. Several times she sank in snow to her knees and imagined her tears turning to pellets of ice that clinked on the hoar and the rocks of the crag.

In her letter to Russell Core just three days after her boy was taken, she wrote that she did not expect to find him alive. A jagged trail of the boy's blood had led from their back porch and through the patchy woods into the hills above. Still, she needed his body, or whatever remained, if only his bones. That's the reason she was writing Core, she said. She needed him to get her boy's bones and maybe slaughter the wolf that took him. No one in the village would hunt the wolves.

"My husband is due back from the war very soon," she wrote in her letter to him. "I must have something to show him. I can't do without Bailey's bones. I can't have just nothing."

* * *

Core was not a man who easily frightened. He'd begun as a nature writer, and in search of a project went north where the gray wolves found him one fall, watched him for a week as he camped and fished there. They trailed him along the river, wanted something from him, though it was not his death, he knew. He imagined they wanted a story woven of truth, not myth, one not tilted by dread. The following winter he journeyed to Yellowstone. His second book chronicled that year of living among the grays—a narrative written in an alien era of youth, so long ago that Core scarcely believed in its reality.

For the afterword he offered an essay on the only recorded wolf attack on a human in the park. A female gray had crept into a campsite and stolen a toddler while the parents slept off champagne. He explained this killing as the result of food shortages, migrating herds of caribou confused by a late winter, heedless human invasion into the domain of the wolf: roads and campsites and oil-starved engines, all of it an affront to the majesty of what once had been. Even his own presence among them was an indignity. He felt that daily. This girl's death was no mystery, no myth. Only elemental. Only hunger.

He was asked to help in the stabbing cold of that morning—the nature writer who had been tent-living among the clan of this killer. He could not say no. His daughter was the same age as the taken girl and his love for her then felt already like loss. The guilt of a father whose work takes him from home. He and the others, the rangers and biologists and camouflaged men, tracked the wolf across twenty square miles over the Northern Range, through Lamar Valley. He rode on a borrowed four-wheeler and was in radio contact with the sniping copters he hated. He sent them false information so they would not find her. Then he rode across the line into Montana where, alone and sickened, he found her and shot her from forty yards on a cattle farmer's ranch. The rifle they'd given him had no kick—it was nothing like the guns he'd fired as a boy, at the range with his father before his father slumped from life.

That morning Core thought his own land-borne bullet more respectful than those from rangers impersonating gods. Through the scope he could see the wolf's white muzzle still sprayed pink with the child's innards. Pieces of yellow pajamas were glued to the dried purple blood just over her flews. Her eyes were golden. Not the glow of red or green as in picture-book terror-wolves, but a dullish, perversely dignified human gold.

You don't see yourself full, Core knew, until you see yourself reflected in the eye of a beast. This task was a test of human dignity, and he had failed.

No one can deceive the eyes of a wolf. They always know. And in this way he came to know her too. He left just after he killed her. This was his book. It began in tribute and ended in slaughter. He'd studied that female gray for a year. He'd named her the name of his daughter.

Examiners found much of the girl mashed inside the digestive tract. "A goddamn murderer," the dead child's parents said of the wolf that robbed her. "A goddamn demon." But Core knew otherwise. The raider, this marauder, thief in the night—she dared to intrude not because it was her wish but because it was her need. Who was the transgressor here? He wanted to scold these parents, insist on a fine for their wanton camping in a restricted dale, for the plastic trash dumped beside their tent, but he could not.

Then he watched over the next decade as the gray wolf was hunted to near-extinction. Those cowards sniping from their copters. He recoiled each time he remembered squeezing the trigger on that adult female with the strands of cloth stuck to the hinge of her mouth. He became a help to Yellowstone reintroduction, penned newspaper editorials about man's hubris, spoke at college symposiums where khaki-clad alumni nodded in agreement, asked him to sign his book and then quickly forgot.

In her letter Medora Slone wrote of Core's book: "You have sympathy for this animal. Please don't. Come and kill it to help me. My son's bones are in the snow."

* * *

He had Medora Slone's letter folded into the pocket of his denim jacket when he arrived at the nursing home, a sprawling one-level building that used to be an elementary school, classrooms converted into bedrooms but the hallways still school-like. A column of lockers still at one end, the fire alarms plate-sized red bells he remembered from his own youth. His wife of thirty-five years lay sleeping where she'd lain for the past thirteen months, only part lucid in a bed after a stroke had cleaved one half of her head. He stood looking at this woman who needed a power no man or god was able to give.

He went to the sink and drank. In the mirror he saw his white mane spilling to his shoulders from beneath a baseball cap, the ruff of white sprouting from his jawline, a chin that seemed elongated. He could not guess when he had gone so wintry, so wolfish. Thirteen months ago, perhaps. Microwave meals twice a day. The uneven sleep of the sick, all the hours of quiet he counted. The wind in winter an almost dulcet guest for the wail it made. Boredom daily morphed to despair and back. Sixty years old this year and he knew he looked eighty. Unable to summon the will even to see a barber.

How many more paintings could he produce of the wolf he'd slain? The walls of his library were already covered with such creations. Always, it seemed, of the same wolf. Always the yellow strands of cloth pasted into her bloodied mouth. He could not paint her back to the living. He could not will his own living back.

Thousands of titles stood in his library, gathered and read over a lifetime. Each morning he'd stand in that space, bracketed by books. Touching, fanning through volumes, smelling the poems in their pages, but without the urge anymore to read. A random stanza or paragraph was all he could manage. That pine desk, where he'd written his own books, had once belonged to his father. The chestnut leather armchair was a gift from his wife after they were married. In the foyer of their house an undusted crucifix kept watch upon galoshes and gloves, a parka and cowl hooked where she had hooked them a winter ago. A WELCOME mat worn down to COME. His painting studio in the attic, once so organized, was now a havoc of canvases and paint tubes, of brushes and easels and drop cloths. The washing machine broke last winter and he left it that way. Through the cotton blanket he felt for his wife's foot and grasped it in some unsure gesture of goodbye. He thought of his estranged daughter, far off in Anchorage, a college history professor, what she would say when she saw him, when he arrived unbidden. He took his duffel bag and went. In the hallway a female attendant in a red sweater wished him a merry Christmas, handed him a candy cane broken at its curve. Core looked at his watch: Christmas was still three weeks away. He'd forgotten about Thanksgiving. In the parking lot of the nursing home, in the day's gaunt sun, sat idling the same white cab that had delivered him.

* * *

Outside the desert city an urgent wind whisked up sand. Dark mustard gusts passed before a buffed sun and looked like blots of insects sent to swarm. Their vehicle made plumes of tawny dust as they sped after a pickup rusted red and packed with men. Perched at the .50-caliber gun, Vernon Slone heard the sand pepper his face mask. This late in the day and the temperature stayed fixed at one hundred.

Back home he knew it was snowing—a winter he would not see. Behind him the city smoldered. If he turned he could behold the smoke and flames of this Gomorrah they'd made. But before him he could see just the windswept sand and the twirling dust of the truck fifty yards ahead. No one was shooting now. No one could see. Every few seconds, between horizontal gusts of sand, Slone spotted the truck's tailgate.

He watched the truck catch the gulley and overturn four times in near silence, in a storm of sand and dust. He'd seen pickups and snow machines flip in fluffed snow the same way: no sound. The men—what faction were they from? what region?—were tossed from the truck's bed like bags of leaves. The truck slid, smashed to a halt on top of them. Some limped from the tinfoil wreck and shot at Slone's vehicle. The lead dinged against the armor.

When the .50-caliber rounds hit them they tore off limbs or else left dark blue holes the size of plums. He fired into those on the fuel-damp sand and those still crammed inside the truck's flattened cab. Their blood burst in the wind as wisps of orange and red. Curious how orange, how radiant blood looks beneath a desert noon, in the dull even tinge of its light.

The truck ignited but did not explode. They let it burn there for fifteen, twenty minutes and then finally approached with extinguishers.

The boy inside was Bailey's age. The unburned skin of his face shone of caramel. Shirtless, without shoes, his feet so singed they seemed melted and remolded—feet fashioned from candle wax. Spalls of rock made piercings in his neck and chin, the jugular ripped unevenly by broken glass, below it a gown of blood to his kneecaps. Slone looked into the liquid gray eyes of the man beside him—a man whose simple name, Phil, did not seem to fit the darkness Slone knew he had within.

Who issues orders here? What foul game's pieces are we? They sat smoking on their vehicle. Slone watched the others search pockets and packs. Some clicked shots of the wreck, showed each other, and laughed. Phil bent to knife out the eyes and tongues of the dead—these would be his keepsake.

* * *

Core arrived in Alaska in the faint hold of early dusk. He'd slept on the flight, was winched down deep into the vagueness of dreams where he saw the bleared faces of his wife and daughter, and of someone else in shadows, someone he suspected was his mother. At the airport he asked a man the way to the rental car counter and the man simply pointed to the sign directly in front of them, the company's name shouting inside a yellow arrow. In a shop he stood before a magazine rack, made-up faces grinning on covers but he could not name a single one. Alaska papers proclaiming weather. He bought a candy bar.

He rented a four-wheel-drive truck to go the one hundred miles inland to the village of Keelut. The truck had a GPS suctioned to the windshield but he'd never used one before, and the attendant told him that where he was going could not be found on GPS. He gave Core a road map, "one of the more accurate ones," he said, and in red marker traced Core's path from the airport to Keelut. But Core was lost immediately upon leaving the terminal, on a road that brought him to the hub of this odd city. He saw bungalows hunkered beside towers, Cessna seaplanes parked in driveways, cordwood piled in front of a computer store. Filthy vagrants loping along with backpacks, groomed suits on cell phones.

When he found the right road the city shrank behind him, the December-scape unseen beyond the green glow of the dashboard. He saw old and new snow plowed into half-rounded wharves along the roadside. The red and white pinpricks of light that passed overhead were either airplanes or space vessels. He felt the possibility of a close encounter with discoid airships, with gunmetal trolls from a far-off realm descending to ask him questions he'd not be able to answer. Half an hour of careful driving and the snow came quick in two coned lanes the headlamps carved from darkness. What would he tell Medora Slone about the wolf that had stolen her child? That hunger is no enigma? That the natural order did not warrant revenge?

He'd seen his daughter only once in the last three years, when she came home the morning after her mother's stroke. Three crawling years. Life was not short, as people insisted on saying. He'd quit cigarettes and whiskey just before she was born. He wanted to be in health for her and knew then that ten years clipped from his life by drink and smoke were ten years too many. Now he knew those were the worthless years anyway, the silver decade of life, a once-wide vista shrunk to a keyhole. Not all silver shines. As of this morning he had plans to return to cigarettes and whiskey both. He regretted not buying them at the airport.

Highways to roads to paths, towns to wilderness, the wider and wider dispersion of man-made light. One lost hour in the opposite direction, in a deepening dark of forest that seemed eager to ingest him. Then a trucker at a fuel station who gave him a better map, who pointed the way, although he wasn't certain, he said. An eagle was tattooed in black above his eye. "I'm just looking for the easiest roads," Core told him, and the trucker said, "Roads? This place doesn't have roads." He laughed then, only three teeth in a mouth obscured by an unruly beard. Core could not understand what he meant. The snow stopped and he drove on.

Hours later, Core made it to an unpaved pass without a mark to name it. This was the pass to Keelut, a right turn where the hills began to rise close to the road, just past a rotted shanty the trucker had told him to watch for. In four-wheel drive he bumped along this pass until he came to the village. He could count the cabins, arranged in two distinct rows. Most were one-level with only a single room. Some were two-level with sharply slanted roofs and radio antennae stretching into the cold. The hills beyond loomed in protection or else threatened to clamp.

He parked and walked in drifts to his shins. Sled dogs lay leashed beside cabins, huskies huddled together and harnessed, white-gray and cinnamon in sudden moonlight, the snow about them flattened, blotched pink and bestrewn with the bones of their supper. Muscled and wolfish, indifferent to this cold, uncaring of him. He was surprised by a child standing alone in the dark. He stopped to look, unsure if she was real, then asked her for the way to the Slones' cabin. This child's cordate face was part Yup'ik, lovely in its unwelcome look. She simply pointed to the cabin before turning, before fleeing into snow-heavy spruce squat in the shadowed dark. He watched her disappear between branches, wondered where she could be going in such chill of night. Why was she not fearful of wolves, of being taken as the others had been taken?

The moon on the snow tricked the eye into seeing the snow itself emanate light. To his left, silhouetted against a sky almost neon blue, stood a totem pole keeping sinister watch at the rim of the village—twenty feet high, it bore the multicolored faces of bears, of wolves, of humanoid creatures he could not name, at the top a monstrous owl with reaching wings and massive beak. He turned to look down the center stretch of the village—not a road but a plowed and shoveled path between two banks of cabins, at the end what seemed a town square with a circular stone structure, half hidden now in hillocks of snow. To his right a wooden water tower with a red-brick base, useless in winter. Behind it a grumbling generator shack giving power to this place. In the orange glow of cabin windows he could spot round faces peering out at him. The air now nearly too cold to breathe.

He walked on to the Slones' cabin. A set of caribou antlers jabbed out from above the door—in welcome or warning, he could not be sure.

* * *

Medora Slone had tea ready when he finally entered. He was surprised by her white-blond youth. He'd expected the dark raiment of mourning and messed black hair. Her face did not fit, seemed not of this place at all. Hers was the pale unmarked face of a plump teenage softball player, not a woman with a dead boy and a husband at war. Her eyes were pale too. In a certain angle of lamplight they looked the sparest sheen of maize, almost gold.

Her cabin at the edge of the village was built better than most. Two rooms, tight at the edges, moss chinking between logs. Half a kitchen squeezed into a corner, a cord of wood stacked by the rear door, fireplace and granite hearth at one end, cast-iron stove at the other. Bucket of kindling near the stove, radio suspended from a nail in a log. He could brush the ceiling with a fingertip. Easier to heat with low ceilings, he knew. Plastic sheeting stapled and duct-taped over windows to keep out cold. A rifle in the umbrella stand, a child's BB gun in a corner. Compound bow and quiver of arrows hung above the hearth. His book on wolves was partially stuffed between two cushions of the sofa, pages folded over and under, the cover torn. He asked to use her bathroom and ignored himself in the glass.

They sat across from one another—she on a sofa whose cushions were worn to the foam, he sunk low in an armchair—and they sipped tea in the quiet welcomed by their exhaustion. She

WILLIAM GIRALDI

offered him the food that others from the village had been bring-
ing to her since her son's disappearance—caribou soup, fry bread,
moose stew, wheat berries, pie baked with canned peaches. But
he had no appetite now. The tea warmed his limbs, a lone orange
coal or glowing hive pulsing from the center of him. He rolled
the sleeves of his flannel shirt. On the pine arm of the chair were
the ring stains of a coffee mug—an Olympic logo warped and
brown.

"*Canis lupus*," she said.

"Yes, ma'am."

"Apex predator." She moved his book to the coffee table
between them. "Ice age survivor from the Late Pleistocene. What's
that mean?"

"It means they've been around a long time and know how to
hunt better than we do."

"You sound . . . happy by that."

"I'm sorry about your son, Mrs. Slone."

"You've come to kill it, then? To kill that animal that took him?"

He looked but did not answer.

"So why'd you come, then? I was a little surprised you replied
to the letter I sent."

The crushing quiet of his house.

"I came to help if I can," he said. "To explain this if I can."

"The explanation is that we're cursed here. The only help is to
kill it."

"You know, ma'am, I'm just a writer."

"You've hunted and killed one of them before. I read that in
your book."

"Where'd you find the book?"

"It found me. I don't know how. It was just here one day."

She looked to the room around them, trying to recognize it, trying to remember.

"You mentioned getting the boy's bones, but . . . I don't know."

"Yes," she said. "I was thinking that his bones would show during breakup."

"Breakup?"

"You know, in spring. After the thaw."

He did not tell her this was impossible. The boy's yellow snow boots stood like sentinels on the mat near the door, his pillowed coat on a hook, but there was no framed school photo grinning at Core gap-toothed from the mantel, no plastic trucks or toy guns on a carpet. If not for the boots and coat, this woman before him was just another story among the many he'd been told. Sixty years old, he was half sure he'd heard every tale worth hearing. That morning at the airport, sitting at a window in a boulevard of sunlight, in spring's cruel tease, he tried to remember his parents' faces and could not.

"I would have killed the thing myself," she said. "If I could have found it. I tried to find it. I tried to do it."

"No, their territory could be up to two hundred square kilometers. It's good you didn't find it. The pack is probably eight or ten members. No more than twelve, I'd guess. You don't want to find that."

"Can I ask you a personal question, Mr. Core?"

He nodded.

"Do you have a child?"

"Yes, a daughter, but she's grown now. In Anchorage, she teaches at the university. I'll see her when I leave here."

"A teacher like her father."

"I'm no teacher. I maybe could have been, but . . . She's good at it, I hear. She wanted to be an Alaskan."

"That city's not Alaska. Where you are right now, Alaska starts here. We're on the edge of the interior here."

He said nothing.

"Mr. Core, do you have any idea what's out those windows? Just how deep it goes? How black it gets? How that black gets into you. Let me tell you, Mr. Core, you're not on Earth here." She looked into the steam of her mug, then paused as if to drink. "None of us ever have been."

He watched her drink. "I've felt that in certain places over the years."

"Certain places. I mean what you feel here won't be the same as anything you've ever felt before."

He waited for an explanation.

She gave him none.

"But this is your home," he finally said.

"I'm not from here originally. I was brought here when I was a child, and that makes me not from here."

"Brought here from where?"

"I don't remember that. I've never been told where and I never asked. But I know this place is different."

He imagined her in the snow standing naked, almost translucent, a vision caught for only a second before blinking her gone. "Yes, ma'am," he said.

Her eyes flicked about the room in anxiety, in expectation. She lifted his book from the table and fanned through the pages. "I don't understand what they're doing here," she said.

"Who?"

"Wolves."

"They've been here for half a million years, Mrs. Slone. They walked over the Bering land bridge. They live here."

They live here. And Core knew they helped rule this continent until four hundred years ago. Inuit hunters learned to encircle caribou by watching wolves. Hunting-man revered another hunter. Farming-man wanted its existence purged. Some set live wolves ablaze and cheered as they burned. *Wolf and man are so alike we've mistaken one for the other:* Lupus est homo homini. *This land has hosted horrors most don't care to count. Wolfsbane. But we are the hemlock, the bane of the wolf.* Core said nothing.

"I don't understand what they're doing *here*," and she gestured feebly in front of her, at the very space on the rug where her son had no doubt pieced together a puzzle of the solar system. Or else scribbled a drawing of the very monster that would one day come for him, stick-figure mother and father looking on, unable to help.

"Why is this happening to me, Mr. Core? What myth has come true in my house?"

"They're just hungry wolves, Mrs. Slone. It's no myth. It's just hunger. No one's cursed. Wolves will take kids if they need to. This is simple biology here. Simple nature."

He wanted to say: *All myths are true. Every one is the only truth we have.*

She laughed then, laughed with her tear-wet face pressed into her hands. He saw her fingernails were gnawed down to nubs. He knew she was laughing at him, at his outsized task here before her.

"I'm sorry," he said, and looked at his boots. "I don't know why this is happening to you, Mrs. Slone."

He could name no comfort for this. His face warmed with the foolishness of his being here.

More quiet. And then: "Does your husband know?"

She seemed startled by the word, unready to recall her husband. "Men were supposed to call him there, to call the ones who could tell him. But I said I would do it, that I should be the one to do it. I never did, though. I can't tell him while he's there. He'll see for himself." She paused and considered her gnawed fingertips. "He'll see what has happened. What we've done. What no one here was able to stop."

"They're hungry and desperate," he said. "They don't leave for the fringes of their territory unless they're desperate. They avoid contact with humans if they can. If we'll let them. The wolves that came to this village must be rabid. Only a rabid or starved wolf does what happened here."

He looked beyond her, looked for the language but it was not there. "The caribou must have left early," he said. "For some reason."

He could have told her more. That wolves have a social sophistication to make many an American town look lagging. That the earliest human tribes were identical to wolf packs. That a healthy gray wolf's yearly requirement of meat can reach two tons, that they'll cannibalize each other, kill their own if the hunger hones to a tip. He'd seen this in the wild. A six-year-old boy would have shredded like paper in the teeth of any adult male. It killed the boy at his throat and then rent through the clothing to get at the belly, its muzzle up beneath the ribs to eat the organs it wanted.

"If I can ask," he said, "why wouldn't anyone here hunt the wolves after what happened?"

"They're afraid. And the ones who don't have fear have respect. They respect the thing. They probably think we deserve it, we deserve what happened here."

"I don't understand, Mrs. Slone."

"Stay here long enough and you might. Can I refill your tea?"

He indicated no. His tea was finished now and he felt the first shadows of sleep drop across his shoulders. Somewhere in the village a brace of sled dogs barked up at constellations stretched across a bowl of black. Both he and Medora Slone turned to look at the sheeted window. Where were the sled dogs when the wolves came? He remembered a Russian proverb: *Do not call the dogs to help you against the wolves.*

He remembered a story he'd been told and could never say if it was parable or fact but he told it to her anyway: "In Russia, during a winter of the Second World War, a food shortage was on. No meat, no grain. The fighting decimated the land. The wolves rampaged into villages and mauled at random. Like they were their own invading army. They killed hundreds of people that winter, and not just women and children. Drunk old men or crippled men too weak to defend themselves. Even dogs. There was nobody left to hunt the wolves. All the able men were at the war or dead. Somehow aware of that imbalance, the wolves came and left scenes of carnage almost as bad as the bombs. Doctors said they were rabid, but the villagers said they were possessed by demons hell-bent on revenge. Their howls, they said, sounded like hurt demons. It was revenge, the old people thought. Revenge for something, for their past, maybe, I don't know."

She stared at him—she didn't understand. She looked insulted.

"I mean you're not alone," he said.

"Yes, I am. What's done can't be undone, can it? Just look what we're capable of, Mr. Core," and she held up her palm for him to see. But he did not know why and was too frightened to ask.

She lowered her hand and said, "Come, I'll show you outside where the children were taken. Are those your boots?"

He looked at his feet. "These are my boots."

"You'll need better boots."

* * *

This stolid village remained gripped in snow and stillness, and over the hills lay a breadth without end, an echoing cold with a mind that won't be known. Yellow-orange squares burned in the sides of log and frame homes, stone spires exhaling wood smoke. From the hook on a cabin hung a fish chain with two silver salmon. Core saw overturned dogsleds and toboggans, canoes and aluminum boats, ricks of exposed wood, pickup trucks with tire chains. Adjacent to some cabins were plywood kennels for sled dogs. Unlabeled fifty-five-gallon drums, rust-colored, most with tops torched off. Shovels and chain saws and snow machines, Coleman lanterns dented and broken. Gas-powered auger to drill lake ice. Blue tarp bungeed around a truck's engine on sawhorses. Vehicles mugged by snow and stranded. The church an unpainted A-frame beside the schoolhouse. And all around, those hills with howls hidden within.

He'd been deep into the reaches of Montana, Minnesota, Wyoming, Saskatchewan, but no place he could remember matched the oddness, the otherness he felt in this place. A settlement at the edge of the wild that both welcomed and resisted the wild.

"It's beautiful here," he said, his words in a cloud. It was a lie, and he knew she heard it as a lie.

She looked to him. "You don't understand."

"What don't I understand, Mrs. Slone?"

She neither tensed against the cold nor appeared to feel the freeze on her naked face and hands.

"This wildness here is inside us," she said. "Inside everything."

She pointed out beyond the hills at an expanse vaster than either of them knew.

"You're happy here?" he asked.

"Happy? That's not a question I ask myself. I see pictures in magazines, vacation pictures of islands, such green water and sand, girls in bathing suits, and I wonder about it. Seems so strange to me, being there. There's a hot spring not so far from here, a three-hour walk, a special place for me, hidden at the far end of the valley. That's as close as I get to warmth and water."

"A hot spring sounds good right now," he said.

"Good to get clean," she said, and he did not ask what she meant by that.

"I've come to help you if I can, Mrs. Slone. Nothing's a novelty to me here."

She wouldn't look at him now. "Mr. Core, my husband left me alone here with a sick child."

"You met in this village?"

"We never met anywhere. I knew him my whole life. Since before my life. I don't have a memory he isn't in. And he left me here."

"But the war."

"I heard on the radio it's not a real war. Someone said that."

"It's real enough, Mrs. Slone. People are dying real deaths. On both sides."

"He said he'd never leave me. That's what men say. Words can't be worthless, just thrown away like some trash. There's punishment for the wrong words."

"But I've found that sometimes life interferes with words. Or changes what you meant by them."

She turned from him and walked on. He followed. From a copse of birch a Yup'ik man and his boy, both with rifles, dragged a lank moose calf, barely meat enough for a family's meal. Medora Slone and Core watched them pull it through the snow to their cabin beyond the copse.

They walked again in silence.

"That's the pond where the first was taken." She pointed.

He wiped his wet nostrils with a glove.

"Didn't you bring some warmer clothes?"

"I didn't expect this kind of cold," he said.

"It's not even cold yet, Mr. Core. I have some warmer clothes for you. And Vernon's good boots."

"You said before your son was sick."

"He wasn't the right one."

"I'm sorry?"

"He stopped going to school after his father left."

"That's normal enough, I think. Children usually don't like school at first. My daughter went through that."

His daughter was of course grown, very much alive, a lifetime of school in her past. He wanted to blame his exhaustion, this ungodly cold for his carelessness, his stumbling words.

"I'm sorry," he said, "I only meant—"

"Stop apologizing to me." She pointed again. "The wolf came from that dip in the hill, at the far side of the pond there. I found its tracks. I followed them. And there was nothing normal about our son."

He saw at the pond the snow-covered rectangle he guessed was a dock. Children leapt from that dock in summer, but imagining the sounds of their splashes was not possible now. This village tableau repelled every thought of summer and light. He wanted to understand what warmth, what newness and growth was possible here, but he could not.

"The second was taken over here. The girl," she said, and they moved around the pond, behind a row of cabins to where the low front hills split to form an icy alcove. "The children sled in here, down that hill there."

He remembered: *Take warning hence, ye children fair; of wolves' insidious arts beware.*

"Bailey too?"

"Bailey didn't sled." She paused here, hand on her womb as if the womb held memory the hand could feel. "He just wasn't the right one."

"I'm not sure what you mean by that, ma'am."

"He didn't sled."

They stood staring into the alcove; he tried to imagine the animal charging down the slope. A startled child's visage of terror. A gust lifted from their left, carried blurs of snow and yanked at their clothes. Medora Slone moved through wind and snow as others move through sun.

"How did it feel to shoot that female wolf?" she asked.

"I was there to study them."

"And you really believe what you wrote? That a wolf taking a child is part of the order of things out there?" She gestured to the hills, past the hills.

"Yes, I do, Mrs. Slone."

"How did it feel to shoot it?"

"I didn't have much of a choice that day. It felt bad."

"But not so rare?"

"Very rare," he said. "They aren't what you think, Mrs. Slone. What happened here does not happen."

She stared—her eyeballs looked frozen. "What happened here happened to *me*."

WILLIAM GIRALDI

He closed his eyes and kept them closed in the cold, loathing the words that might come from him. He said nothing.

"I suppose you're hungry now," she said. "I have some soup for you."

When they arrived back at the Slones' front door, he asked, "Where was your son taken?"

"Around back," she said, and gestured feebly with her chin at the corner of the cabin.

"May I see?"

"I'd rather you didn't now," she said, and took his gloved hand to lead him inside, a lover's gesture he could not make sense of.

She heated caribou soup in a small dented pot on the burner. In the armchair he ate from the pot and let the broth transform him, quash his ability to fend off this insistent sleep. She traded him a mug of black coffee for the pot. He saw on a shelf a half-gone bottle of whiskey and asked if she might add some to his coffee. She poured into his mug and when he drank the heat of it filled the hollowness in him.

He asked then if she might have a cigarette and chocolate. From a cupboard she retrieved them, an unopened bag of chocolate he knew must have belonged to the boy, and a brand of filterless cigarettes he did not recognize. They sat and smoked together but they did not speak. His chest and lungs felt aflame at first, but after several pulls they remembered. He smoked smoothly with the chocolate smeared to the roof of his mouth and was thankful for this pleasure among so much sting.

She rose to answer a knock on the rear door. It was the boy of the Yup'ik hunter they'd seen earlier; he handed her an unwrapped slab of the moose calf, no larger than her palm, and she thanked him.

When she returned to the sofa Core said, "The others here love you."

"No," she said. "It's not love. It's just what we do. Everyone shares with everyone."

"It's not common where I'm from."

"I left a quilt and pillow here for you, Mr. Core. I see you're tired." She rose from the sofa and placed her mug on the counter-top. "Thank you for coming here. I can't pay you anything."

"It's all right," he assured her.

"Is your daughter expecting you?"

"I'm not sure what she expects, actually. I might call when I'm done here. Or just go. Thank you for the soup and coffee."

She fed the fire wedges of axed wood. "You'll get cold in the night when this fire dies. That heater there works, when the electric works. You're free to use it, just roll it to you. Or I can start up the stove for you."

"I'm all set," he said.

"Good night, Mr. Core."

She clicked off the lamp before turning into the back room. "To bed, to bed," he heard her say, and the door clicked shut.

* * *

In the dark beneath the quilt he felt the fissure filling in him, sleep his sole respite against the strafing day. He was still disoriented in this place; he wanted badly to remember where he came from, and why he had come.

He heard the howl of a wolf seconds before sleep would drag him down into darkness. It was mournful through the iced black of night—an uncommon howl, an appeal he could not identify: part

33

fury, part fear, part puzzlement. The female gray he had tracked and killed so long ago howled at him—he knew the howl was at him—from across three miles of flat expanse, from the center of that stripped abundance.

Many nights he expected to be jarred awake by dreams of the wolf he'd killed, by the sharp crack of the rifle round. And when he slept soundly through till dawn, he woke feeling remorseful that his rest had not been disrupted.

With sleep wafting in now he thought he heard the mutters of Medora Slone from the back room, the incantations of a witch, songs whispered through sobs. He knew what haunted meant. The dead don't haunt the living. The living haunt themselves.

An hour into sleep, somewhere at the heart of an errant dream, he woke to light knifing out from around the bathroom door, to the sound of water running into the tub. He sat up on the sofa and listened. She had not closed the door completely, and in his wool socks, slick on the wood floor, he crept to look, terrified by what he was doing, by the chance of being seen by her, but helpless to ignore this. He could hear her muttering, and when he crouched by the door and looked into the crack of light, he saw her sitting in the steam of the tub, scrubbing herself raw with a bath brush, her expression one of pained resolve. Ashamed, he returned to the sofa and raised the quilt to his chin.

But soon he woke again, and he saw the naked figure of Medora Slone silhouetted before the window. She'd pulled away the plastic sheeting and stood now motionless with her hand on the glass opaque with rime, moon-haunted, it seemed to Core, but there was no moon anymore. The firelight had died and the blue-white night was unnaturally intense around her. He saw the folds of her waist, the weighted breasts falling to either side of her rib cage, the tiny cup of flesh at her elbow. He lay unmoving in a kind of fear looking at her over his cosseted body, his breath stifled lest she hear him watching, lest he disrupt this midnight vigil.

"Is he up there? Or down there?" Her voice, no more than a murmur, came to him as if from across an empty chamber.

"Mrs. Slone? It's late, Mrs. Slone. Are you all right?"

She turned to see him lying on the sofa. He could make out only half her face. If he sat up he could reach over the cushioned arm and stroke her hip, her breast, no more than a yard away.

He rose to stack more wood in the hearth, then wheeled the electric heater near the sofa. When she moved toward him, he instinctively peeled back the quilt and shifted to make room. She fit into him imperfectly, the sofa sank more, then he covered them in the quilt and clutched her quaking body.

With her back to him, she took his hand and brought it to her throat, folding it hard around her windpipe, trying to will his grip to squeeze. He tried to retrieve his hand but she held tighter, then slid it down and placed it between her thighs, on a woolly patch of yellow hair. Arms around her again, he held her till she passed into the twitch of a nightmared sleep.

II

On patrol through the western sector of the city Vernon Slone saw pyramids of tires flaming on street corners in their own weather of black smoke. A market bombed and abandoned, fruit on the stones like vivisected bellies, the buildings behind the market reduced to irregular mounds of rubble, some of them unrecognizable as former houses or places of ware. Another afternoon's creep, the cool of dusk an impossibility only dreamed of.

Their vehicle crawled and stopped and crawled again, not knowing where it wanted to be in a spread-out train of trucks snaking through these streets. First his wishes of being in the snowed-over scape he knew, then his teary-eyed vision from the fires. He searched for movement, for men among the wreckage, anything with life left to end. On the road the top half of a man's charred body, snipped through at the waist, entrails in a fly-feasting pile, his one arm outstretched as if trying to swim the torso back to his bottom part.

And then the rapid snaps from rifles on a rooftop. Or from the maw in a bombed building. He knew that one round had entered his right shoulder, had just missed his vest. He could feel the blood, the heated honey in his armpit hair. An explosion from under the vehicle in front of his. It lifted sideways from force of flame and burned there in front of him. A soldier on fire limped from the wreck, one arm missing like the jagged end of driftwood, his other waving somebody to come near, to extinguish this new thing upon him. But no one came and he dropped to burn in the road.

Slone scattered the .50-caliber rounds into bricks, into doors, into a disabled pickup with a missing front axle. Movement on a roof and he fired there. A face-wrapped man with a rifle darted from behind the abandoned pickup and tried to make the alleyway. Slone hit him before he reached it. The rounds punched his back and split his head, strewed the beige building with a flare of red. For an instant it looked to Slone almost like a painting, the lustrous spray of it something he once saw in an art book.

The other gunners in his line of trucks were unloading now in a din of machine gun fire. To his right behind a mound of rubble, another face-wrapped man. Slone trained on him as he moved, the rounds hacking off pieces of him as if from axe blows.

The burst in his neck then felt like the release of steam or gas— not even a spark of pain. When he slumped down expecting the mantle of black, he thought of Bailey in front of a television: *Dad, look at this, look*, and on the screen were trapeze artists breaking free of gravity, soaring, their bodies unnaturally elastic but strong. And then the trapeze artists were gone, the tent's top blew off, dispensed in smoke, and the boy's face turned an iced-over blue, mouthing slow words to Slone he could neither hear nor lip-read. But he imagined his son saying *Remember me* and he tried to reach out for the boy but could not.

Some time later—he couldn't tell how long, each minute a grain of sand dropping in an hourglass—he awoke on a gurney, worked on by others, rough hands mending his shoulder and neck, a corporal grinning down, "You lucky fucker, you're going home." His said his son's name and the corporal told him, "Soon, you lucky fucker, you'll see him soon." The small-caliber round had missed both his pharynx and spine.

"Nothing but a hickey, man," someone said, and he felt the pinch of a syringe and sleep then lowered him into a grateful dark where he could not dream.

*　*　*

Core woke in this winter dark before a belated dawn, Medora Slone still asleep and nude beside him on the sofa, the electric heater and their bodies an able source of warmth, the quilt a caul he wanted to remain in. Soon he built a fire, started the woodstove. She dressed and cooked and watched him depart with the AR-15 rifle and a pack of provisions and snowshoes. He wore her husband's boots and one-piece of caribou hide—a winter suit she'd crafted herself for the unholiest cold. She covered the end of the rifle barrel with masking tape. Core asked her why.

"To keep snow out of the gun," she said.

"I won't get snow in the gun."

"You will when you fall."

"I'm not planning to fall."

"Everyone falls in the snow, Mr. Core. If you feel yourself starting to sweat, rest until you're dry."

"What's wrong with sweat?"

"Nothing till you're wet through. Wet and it freezes to your skin when you stop moving."

"I've been in the cold before," Core said.

"Not like the cold that's coming here."

She opened the door for him and he stepped outside, his face angled up into the flakes falling slant the size of quarters. She remained against the doorframe and tied her robe closed.

"I thought it might be too cold to snow," he said.

"What's that mean?" she asked.

"Too cold to snow. I've heard that. Though I've never understood it."

"Maybe where you come from. But here it's never too cold to snow. There's something off, something wrong with the sky here."

Core looked up into the dark, looked for whatever it was she might have meant.

"Do you know if the snow is coming heavy today?"

"I don't tell the weather, Mr. Core. It will tell me."

Core thanked her, left her framed in a soft glow at the door of her cabin.

He saw the lightening sky through a splayed reach of trees. At the perimeter of the village, in the copse near the hill where the path wound up and around, he suddenly spotted a back-bent Yup'ik woman with a circular face burning items in a rusted drum.

He glimpsed her through the spiderweb of tree limbs and twigs. He stopped on the path to see if she would notice him. When she did she waved him over to the fire. He saw the red-orange radiance on her jowls, her creature garment thick and soiled, pungent-looking in the firelight, an anorak a century old. Her feet and shins were sheathed in moose-hide mukluks. He could not tell what blazed in the drum. He guessed she was burning household trash, but why at this dead hour? Seniors the world over woke before first light as if to win some contest with the sun.

She said, "I thought you were something wicked coming my way."

"No, ma'am," he said. "I'm heading into the hills."

She had a man's voice, teeth missing. "To get a wolf's tooth, I've been told."

"Yes," he said. "How do you know?"

"We're a small village. We've had trouble enough here."

"The wolves. I know, ma'am. I'm sorry."

"Ah, you know? No, you think you do. I mean trouble since the start. Trouble before any of us was here. You would bar the door against the wolf, why not more against beasts with the souls of damned men, against men who would damn themselves to beasts? Answer that."

"I'm sorry, ma'am?"

"I read the books they bring me. What else to do here through nights like these? I read the books. The Christians came when I was a child. The missionaries. They taught me the books. They came with books and they came with the plague."

"I'm sorry?"

"The influenza plague."

The flame widened in the barrel and Core could feel its broad heat from six feet away.

"Do you know the name of this village?" she asked.

"Keelut."

"Say its meaning."

"I don't know its meaning."

"Its meaning is an evil spirit disguised as a dog. Or a wolf."

"Why would they name it that?" he asked.

Her gums glowed part orange, part pink. "Why indeed. You are the wolf expert, I hear."

"My name is Core."

"That girl knows this place is cursed."

"The girl? Medora Slone?"

"Her."

"She just lost her child. What she knows is grief."

"Will the wolves come again for us tonight?"

"Wolves should not be coming here at all. Tonight or ever."

"I did not say *should*. I said *will*." She stared. "They have the spirits of the damned."

"They're hungry wolves, hungry animals. Nothing more."

"I don't mean wolves."

"I'll go now," he said.

"Beware of false prophets, which come to you in sheep's clothing, but inwardly they are ravening wolves."

"That's the Gospel of Matthew."

"I told you, I can read the books. They taught me how."

"Why did you say that?"

"Are you a Christian?"

"Ma'am, I know some things about nature and wolves. I write about them. I don't pretend to know about anything else."

"We all pretend. And they know about you too."

"I'll go now," he said. He made to move up the trailhead. "Have a good day, ma'am."

"You're going the wrong way," she said, not turning her face from the heat of the drum. "Go back the way you came," and she pointed a bent finger to the snow-blown center of the village.

Core ignored her and continued up the path, over chokes of rock and lightning-struck spruce.

* * *

He expected to find a wolf pack in the valley on the other side of these hills, a den tucked away, hidden on a bouldered ridge above the plain. He'd meet them just after daybreak at the den, if he could find it, meet them after their long night hunting afield. If there was a famine on this land, they'd have to seek their prey at the edges of the land they knew.

He remembered telling his daughter this when she was a girl: the Apache hunted the wolf as a rite from boy to man. A wolf kill turned a teen into a leader and earned him favor with the spirits of his ancestors. He remembered being outraged when she brought home from grade school the children's book *Peter and the Wolf*, how it painted the animal a hellish fiend. And now Core was hunting one for a reason and a woman he did not know.

The boy's bones would not be in the den; it had been twelve days since he was taken. His bones were spread throughout this wilderness by scavengers, blanketed by mantles of new snowfall. There would be no burial, no coming to terms for the woman and her husband. But he would kill an already half-dead wolf if he could. He would carry it back for Medora Slone, tell her it was the monster that had seized her son. The monster she wanted to believe in, to explain this away. A wolf's corpse meant relief to her—but only the illusion of relief, he knew. Perhaps she'd be able to quit the midnight vigils knowing that one wolf had been removed from the world. Perhaps not. Her every day was a midnight now.

He trundled through drifts to his shins despite these snowshoes. The sack of food and ammunition hung heavy on his shoulders. The snow ceased briefly beneath a clearing sky to the east. The coming dawn cast a half halo of light on the horizon, then clouds like great coats hurled in to cloak it. Year's end at this latitude the sun rose and set in such a truncated arch it seemed it might not find the will to bring the day.

He felt again the weight in his legs. Beyond the snowed-in trees, just over these hills, lay an unknowable compass of tundra, a tapestry of whites and grays. Everywhere the living cold. Like grief, cold is an absence that takes up space. Winter wants the soul and bores into the body to get it. What were the possibilities of this place? There were patterns hidden here beneath the snow, patterns knowable but he did not know them.

He walked on from one bluff to the next, knoll to knoll, snow-shoeing over nonexistent paths and seeking tracks. The horizon kept losing its line, mixing down with up. Hours into his trek over the hills he stopped under a rock face, alongside what seemed an ancient esker. A minor sun drained of color blinked on and off behind clouds. The uniform white on the land pained his eyes until he remembered the tinted goggles in his bag. While drinking from snow and eating an egg sandwich she'd made for him, he heard the first howls down in the valley, half a mile over the tallest crest in the hills. He had seen no caribou tracks, no coyotes, no lynx, not a moose or hare.

What plague had invaded these vast silences? The virid earth, his memories of fruit breathing hotly in summer fields—all obliterated by this moonscape.

He felt the food warm in him and walked onto the snow-steamed plain. The wind flogged him, rushed around his hood, pushed against the padded contours of his clothes, made chalk dust of air. He adjusted the goggles on his face and tugged his chin low into the ruff of Vernon Slone's caribou suit. It seemed he'd have to walk a long while more. He looked to the sky but could not tell time from a sun this sick. The bluff ahead was at two hundred yards, or three hundred, or three-quarters of a mile—this land made measurement obsolete. Only a fool counted steps and yet he counted. The goggles kept clouding and he stopped to wipe them dry.

Where the plain began to rise again into an escarpment he found the first lupine tracks, a male, nearly six inches around, a three-foot stride, a hundred and twenty pounds, he guessed. He climbed the bank, over half boulders on the talus, and mounted the ridge from a narrow pass, all bluff face below him now, clouds gone north again. To his right he saw steam escaping from a copper-colored mouth in the crag, perhaps the hot spring she had told him about the night before. The sun sat low and wide; snow gave the glimmer of rattled foil. He crouched at the ridgeline and watched the valley beyond, and there he spotted the pack against the facing hills, a frenzy of ten gray wolves.

Through the field glasses he could see an infant wolf or coyote at the core of this ruck, teeth hooked into its flesh, the two largest wolves rending, angling for leverage, their hackles raised, the bounty shorn between them, snow mottled in purple and red. Core crouched there a long while looking.

He stepped sideways down the escarpment and lost his footing in the snow, then slid several meters until he stopped against a boulder. He sidestepped again the rest of the way until he again met the talus at the plain. There he crouched again and watched through the glasses as the rout of wolves consumed the last of the carcass. He checked to make certain the rifle's magazine was full, then loaded the first round into the chamber, the safety switch still engaged. He set off slowly across the valley floor, the crimped surface hoar crunching underfoot as if it were in pain. He lost sight of the wolves for a time but knew when the wind shifted west his scent would lift and reach them. He was afraid with every step in this snow, aware of the loaded rifle on his shoulder.

On a healthy day in a healthy land the wolf will run from man, turn at first sniff or glimpse—they want nothing of men. But he'd witnessed them prey on bison and caribou, a brigade of only four grays defeating five hundred pounds of beast with a lethal rack of talons. This was what he wanted for himself, he guessed. Unmanning, dismantling. *A body for a body*. Why come all this way for a bereaved woman he'd never met? Why then this futile hunt? He thought of the cigarettes and chocolate, of her scent on the sofa.

He could have ended himself at home. A pistol or rope. A razor. Or pills if he lost all nerve. Or his truck running in the shut garage, garden hose duct-taped to the tailpipe. But the almost pleasant nightmare that had played through his mind the night before he received Medora Slone's letter showed his lax body rent by wolves in an ice-blue scape he could not name. Her letter was the summons he wanted, the sentence that should have come long before. And his daughter in the city here? She was only the daylight reason. He'd never seen a daylight detail that could compete with midnight's verity. The predawn dark never learned to lie.

He walked on and topped the last small crest in the plain. The wind lifted his scent and in minutes the pack knew he was there. From a quarter mile off the wolves stared, their snouts to the air. Core stopped to stare back. He took several steps and stopped again. They looked stymied by confusion, bereft of their instinct to flee. Still they stared, tails raised. He walked toward them.

And they began their charge then, half head-on, the other half split on each flank. They'd surround him, he knew—he'd seen them do it. He dropped to one knee, pulled off a glove with his teeth, and stayed there in wait with the rifle aimed at the alpha out front, a male no more than six, a hundred and twenty-five pounds—it should have been heavier. Take it down, he knew, and the others would lose their will.

The white dust of trampled snow rose among the pack, glittered in broad frames of sun through an open stitch of cloud. Was this the wolf that took the children of Keelut, this deep silver gray with a gloss of cinnamon and that faultless stride?

He centered the wolf's skull in the crosshairs of the scope. In a minute or less the pack would be at him, the alpha ripping his throat, the others threshing at his limbs. Laudable teamwork. They knew his disease of spirit, his want of this. Or else in their own disease mistook him for something other than a man.

He imagined slow-motion and no sound. He knew they must be mad to charge him this way, must be only days away from starving. He unsquinted and lowered the rifle, then let them come to him. This was penance, he knew. The silence of his living room, the thought of painting another oil portrait of the female gray he'd shot, the nightly whirring of his microwave—all an anguish he could not abide, already a death. Most of him wanted this reckoning. Some of him didn't. And he let them come.

When at the last instant he raised the rifle again and fired at the air above the alpha's skull, the pack halted at the crack of the round and glanced to one another. They knew the sound. When they neither advanced nor retreated, another shot above their skulls scattered them west from where they had come at the far end of the valley. He watched them go. He felt nearly surprised at his lack of tears. For the last year he'd imagined this moment a tearful one.

He stood and watched until they were gone. He'd return to Keelut now. He would tell Medora Slone that the wolves were fled from here. Remind her that what was done could not be undone, that blood does not wash blood. She'd have to live on with her lot. He knew no other way.

*　*　*

He trekked back through the late morning and afternoon, the day stiffened and already falling toward dark. He rested when he could, a long spell on the talus after the plain. He packed snow into an aluminum thermos and slipped it inside the caribou one-piece—the clothing of Vernon Slone, he could not forget. Then he sat in a crack in a ridge, safe from the wind. He ate the mixed nuts and ribbons of dried meat Medora Slone had also prepared for him. He thought of sleep. When the snow melted in the thermos he drank it, and then he packed more.

The walking began to feel automatic after that, his legs propelled by an engine wholly apart from him. He thought not of warmth or meal, wife or daughter, only of each step and then the next until he forgot to think about even those. And he walked on like that through the scanting light of day.

When he arrived back at the cabin his lungs felt weighted with rime. Medora Slone did not answer his knock. When he entered he saw her bedroom door ajar, clothes spilling from a closet and strung along the carpet—jeans, sweaters, a negligee of green lace. A suitcase with a cracked handle lying on its side. He called her name. The cold still infused his face; fatigue moved in surges through his limbs.

Weak light knifed through from beneath the narrow door that last night he had thought was a closet. When he opened it a chill hastened up from a never-finished root cellar. The rounded steps had been fashioned from available rock, the sharply slanted ceiling so low he had to duck to clear his head—a stairwell designed for storybook dwarves. A bare lightbulb lit this cramped space. The scent of soil and rock. Crates on an earthen floor. Mason jars of dried food he could not identify. Lumber and visqueen stacked in a corner. Rodent droppings on the dirt.

His breath hung before him as he moved beneath the bulb. Stones had long ago been dislodged from this wall beside the steps. A nook had been carved into the earth with a shovel or pickaxe.

The bulb's weak light did not reach here. He removed a glove to dig free his lighter from a pocket. He moved nearer. Inside this space he saw the boy—the frozen body of the six-year-old Bailey Slone leaning against the earth, cocooned in plastic, his open eyes iced over, mouth ajar as if exhaling—as if attempting a final word of protest.

He would rest here now for some time, sitting in the corner on an overturned Spackle bucket, his legs and back already sore from the hunt. At the airport the day before he'd read in an article that the cosmos consisted mostly of what we cannot see, energy and matter averse to light. He believed this though it sounded insane. He remembered then his hand around the throat of Medora Slone, how she had begged for a punishment, a purifying she could not grant herself.

III

Russell Core hollered down the center stretch of Keelut, his legs wasted from the day's long trek. He pounded madly on doors at dinnertime, shouted his breath onto the frosted glass of windows. The villagers came slowly, warily from their cabins, out into the road, some with rifles, others with lanterns in hand. Some still chewing food, evening fires at their backs. Some holding toddlers who looked upon him with dull suspicion, their ochre skin lovely in the lantern light. All emerged to see this wolf-man messenger Medora Slone had hailed, to confront the sudden roar he'd brought to their night.

"The boy," he yelled. "The boy. Bailey Slone." He pointed behind him toward the dark, told them all the boy was dead, frozen in the root cellar. Most seemed not to understand, or not to want to.

A man they called Cheeon—Vernon Slone's lifelong friend, he'd later learn—rushed past him with a rifle, in untied snow boots and a flannel shirt, in dungarees that had been mended with myriad patches from other denim. Others followed him. Core stayed, bent and panting with hands on knees, attempting to recall the exact age his father fell from cardiac arrest.

When he regained half his breath and straightened in the road, he saw her there at the edge of a cabin less house than hut—the shrunken Yup'ik woman he'd encountered before dawn that morning. He limped to her, his left leg tingling from fatigue, his bared hands beginning to numb. Where were his gloves? He'd left them in the root cellar by the corpse of the boy.

"You knew this morning," he said. "You knew. When we spoke this morning. You knew what she did to the boy."

She only stared.

"You knew," he said.

"What can an old woman know?"

"How could you not say something?"

Above them a makeshift streetlamp throbbed with weakened light, fangs of ice hanging from its shade. The old woman smelled of wood smoke and something foul.

"Go back," she said. "Leave this village to the devils. Leave us be."

Core thought to grab her arm, to lead her to the Slones' cabin to see the boy, to make her understand. But she turned, and on a shoveled path through snow she wobbled behind her hut and dissolved into darkness.

He remained beneath the lamp wearing the one-piece caribou suit and boots that belonged to Vernon Slone. More villagers hurried past him, some saying words he did not know. A snow machine screamed by, its one headlamp coning into the black. He could smell its gasoline fumes in the cold. He tried to follow but his legs wouldn't work and he sat in the road hearing himself breathe. Beguiled by this climate. Terrified of the facts he'd found and fearing already that he could not explain them.

When he reached the Slones' cabin he wedged through the villagers amassed at the door. The whispers he heard had no tone he could name and he wondered if they were accusations against him. In the root cellar, Cheeon had taken the boy from his tomb, untangled the cellophane from him, laid him on the earth floor. He and others were kneeling by the body, afraid, Core thought, to look at one another. A washed-out bruise coursed across the boy's throat and Core knew then he'd been strangled.

In the stagnant cold of that cramped space he heard himself say, "Where is she?"

When no one responded, he asked again, "Where is Medora Slone?"

Cheeon turned to him but would not answer. A brailled scar made a backslash from the corner of his mouth. His black hair was gripped at the nape by a length of clothesline rope. Core could not say what spoke in this man's face—it seemed some mix of boredom and rage. Cheeon said words in Yup'ik to the teen kneeling beside him, then took his rifle from the top of a crate and elbowed past others on the steps. Some remained kneeling by the body but then they too went.

Alone again with the boy, Core felt a kind of vertigo from the sight of him. Children are full of questions but they do not question their own being, are not troubled by their own living. Like animals, they cannot conceive of their mortality. Living seems to them the most natural state of things. But infants, he remembered, were repelled by the elderly, howled in the arms of the olden, as if they could sense, could smell the elderly's proximity to decay.

Core saw a woolen blanket inside a crate and used it to cover the boy. He remained there by him for many minutes, attempting to remember prayers he'd discarded long before this night.

Upstairs in the front room of the cabin again, he waited for someone to speak to him. Perhaps to comfort him. But the villagers only whispered among themselves. Most were Yup'ik, some were white, some mixed. All regarded him with an anxiety that felt both personal and old. Their clothing clashed; one woman wore animal-hide pants and a red jacket with the embossed name of a football team. Core somehow understood that police had been summoned from town, an hour's drive, longer in this snow and dark.

He looked to the whiskey on the shelf, then drank to let it tamp the dread in him. Where were the cigarettes Medora Slone had given him last night? He sank into the same armchair he'd sat in when he arrived the night before. Still no one would speak to him.

He'd never had trouble comprehending how people are what they are. If you live long enough, he knew, you see that the natural world matches the human one. Most are pushed on by appetites no more complicated than a wolf's. A wolf expelled from its pack will travel hard distances to find another—to be accepted, to have kin. It wants to stanch hunger, sleep off fatigue, make itself anew. He understood that. But Medora Slone. How could he explain this? Why did these people refuse to acknowledge him? They began leaving the cabin by twos and did not come back.

He creaked from the armchair to take another pull of whiskey, alone now in the Slones' cabin. At the open front door he squinted out into a mass of ebon silence and could not fathom where these people had gone. Shouts came from somewhere in the village. The barking of sled dogs. Another snow machine screaming through trees. When the wind lifted it carried clouds of snow into the cabin and Core closed the door. He built a hasty fire in the hearth, half surprised he could do it with hands so shaky.

He unpeeled the caribou suit from himself and returned to the armchair, woozy from two pulls of whiskey. From the day's long hunt. He thought of water and food but couldn't move. The heat of the fire flared against his face and he thought then of the husband, of Vernon Slone. Of how these facts would reach him. Of how a husband and father is ravaged by this.

And what he remembered before he blinked into sleep was his own father just after his mother had left the family for reasons no one knew. Ten years old, Core had thought his father would retreat into drink or Jesus. But instead he went to the cinema every night, that one-screen theater with the neon marquee in their nothing Nebraska town. Oftentimes he stayed in the theater to watch the same movie twice—*Spartacus*, *Exodus*, *Psycho*. Core would walk down to Main and Willow to search for him after dark. He'd steal into the exit door of the theater and find his father there—alone before those colossal talking faces, snoring in the chair with an empty bucket of popcorn aslant on his lap.

* * *

Police were in the Slones' cabin now, three white men wearing civilian clothes, winter hunting garb. Upright in the armchair, Core woke to the sound of their wet boots grating against the wood floor. He'd been asleep nearly two hours, he thought, maybe more. He wiped the spittle that had run into his beard, then stood to speak to the man who looked in command, the one with the crew cut, the russet beard, the cigarette behind his ear.

Donald Marium introduced himself to Core; he had the soft hand of a barber and beneath his beard a creaseless face. Core spoke too quickly—who he was, why he'd come, what he'd found—

and Marium told him to sit, to breathe. He went with the two others into the root cellar to see the boy, and minutes later came back to Core, told him to begin his story, to begin where it began. They sat at the table and smoked.

When Core finished his telling, Marium said, "Tell me again, please, why she asked you here."

"I don't know that. She'd read my book on wolves." He glanced about the room for his book but could not see it. From the pocket of his flannel shirt he took the letter Medora Slone had written him and passed it across the table to Marium, who read it in silence.

"And you decided to come here why?"

"To help," Core told him. "She said wolves had taken children from this village. It's in the letter. See for yourself. She said no one would help. I came here to help."

"Wolves did take two kids from here last month. They weren't found. We came here to try and help these people, but I'm not sure how anybody can help that. You can't just walk onto the tundra looking for wolves."

"But no wolf took Bailey Slone," Core said.

Marium flattened his filter into an ashtray, then stood back from the table. Core did the same.

"We'll have to get it all figured out."

"Are the others on their way?" Core asked.

"The others who?"

"The others. The police to find Medora Slone. Shouldn't there be more men here? Investigators? The TV shows have investigators."

"Investigators? Mr. Core, things don't happen here the way they happen anywhere else. And definitely not on TV."

"No investigators? Just you?"

"For now. You have to understand where you are. We don't

have full membership to the rest of the world. And we mostly like it that way. But let's take one thing at a time, please."

"What time is it? Midnight?" His watch was missing from his wrist.

"It's six o'clock, Mr. Core. You're not acclimated here. You said it was just dark when you arrived back here today? That was three-thirty, then."

"That can't be. I left before dawn. I wasn't gone for so many hours." He felt at his left wrist as if he could rub his watch back onto it.

"Dawn is at ten a.m. now, Mr. Core. You're not acclimated here."

"My watch is missing. I don't understand."

"Apparently a woman is missing too."

Core sat again. "I tried to talk to these people but they wouldn't talk to me. Did they tell you anything?"

"Nothing much. Not yet," Marium said. "We spoke to some outside. As you saw, they don't talk much to anyone who isn't one of their own. Let's go back down to see the boy."

In the root cellar the men clicked photos of the body on the floor, of the cavity clawed into the earth. The fat one scratched in a notepad; another with a mustache stood before a laptop on a crate. Core pointed, explained how he'd found the boy, that the man called Cheeon had removed him from the hole and unwrapped him from the plastic sheeting.

"He was upright in there?" Marium asked. "Wedged in?"

Core nodded. "Look at his throat," he said. "She strangled him."

"Someone did."

"It was her," Core said.

"One thing at a time, please, Mr. Core. When you came back here today after your hunt she was gone?"

"She was gone. Look at her bedroom, the back room up there. She packed. Her truck is gone. She's gone. She must have left me here to find the boy."

"Left you here to find the boy. Why would she do that, Mr. Core?"

"Why? Are you the police? You tell me why."

"We'll find out why. We'll get everything figured out."

"Someone has to tell the father," Core said.

"Vernon Slone is at the war."

"You know Vernon Slone?"

"If you live around here, you know of Vernon Slone."

"Someone has to tell him," Core said.

"Would you mind waiting upstairs please, Mr. Core? I'm sorry to ask that. Would you mind?"

"I put that blanket on him," he said, and did not move. "I covered him."

"We'll take care of this boy," Marium said. "Don't you worry. We'll take good care of this boy."

Core made to leave.

"And, Mr. Core?" Marium said. "Please just have a seat up there. Please don't touch anything."

Core went upstairs to the armchair and sat on his hands.

* * *

Hours later Marium and the men laid Bailey Slone in the bed of a police pickup. They walked cabin to cabin throughout the village, looking for the parents of Medora and Vernon Slone. Core remained by the police truck in the road and watched them, smoking from Marium's pack, taking sips of whiskey when the cold cut through him. Keeping solemn watch over the boy.

Retreating to the Slones' cabin to feed the fire when he could bear no more cold.

In the back room he looked at the messed bed of Medora Slone, the boy's tiny bed beside it, on the sheets superheroes faded from washing. He kept rubbing his wrist for the missing watch, kept feeling turned-around without knowing the time.

When Marium finally returned, Core was almost asleep again in the armchair.

"I'm going back to town," he said. "My guys are staying here. You should follow me back, to a motel there. It's way too easy to get lost in the night. And more snow's coming soon. You can't stay here."

"Why not?"

"It's better you don't."

"But why?" Core said. "These people think I have something to do with this?"

"I didn't say that. But you can't stay here."

"What'd you find?"

"Nothing yet."

"Her parents? Or the husband's parents?"

"Nothing yet. Follow me back."

"No one knows anything?" Core said.

"We'll know something soon."

Core started his truck, let the engine warm, saw his breath frozen on the windshield from the day before. For sixty slow miles he stayed trained on the taillights of Marium's truck, two eyes ashine on a face of unbroken black. He fought to keep his own vehicle from slipping across unplowed roads, fought to stop sleep from slamming onto him. The window half open to let the frozen air slap him awake. The radio loud, an upset singer complaining of heart pain. Hard to tell how close the hills and trees came to the road. Impossible to know if there were humans in that darkness. He remembered nothing of this route from the day before.

At this hour of night he could have no accurate notion of the town. He'd expected some lesser oasis at the center of this dead world but the town seemed barely that. In its sickly fluorescent light the motel beckoned from the road without a sign to welcome. He followed Marium into the parking lot, then went to his driver's window to cadge a cigarette.

"How long you staying?"

"I don't know," Core said. "How long should I?"

"A few days, I'd say. At least. Until we get this figured. You can't remember anything she said to you about where she might go to?"

"She didn't say anything to me about leaving. We talked about wolves and we talked about this place. That's all."

"You're sure she did this, but tell me how."

"With a rope. I don't know."

"I don't mean what'd she do it with. I mean *how*."

"I'm not prepared for this, Mr. Marium. You have to talk to the people of that village."

"A tiny old woman came to me when I arrived tonight, as soon as I got out of my truck. She was just standing there. She told me Medora Slone was possessed by a wolf demon. She called it a *tornuaq*. That's what you get when you talk to the people there."

"I'm not prepared for this."

"You see this main road out here?" He pointed with his cigarette. "Our station is at the end of it, on the left down there. Across from the market. Come talk tomorrow please. You should go catch some sleep now."

But sleep would not come. He stretched on the bed in this dank room, hungry without the energy to eat. And he imagined Medora Slone's face in the dark above him. He remembered the flesh of her from the night before, her naked form quaking against his own body.

He could name the facts of nature.

A quarter of all lion deaths are the result of infanticide. A male bass will eat his offspring if they don't swim away in time.

Female swine and rabbits will stifle their young if the young are sick or weak, if resources run low. It's called "savaging."

Prairie dogs kill so many of their own young it's practically a sport for them.

Rats eat their own young if they are hurt or deformed. But they are rats.

Wasps. Sand sharks. Sea lions. Tree swallows.

Those dolphins we so admire for their intelligence: they've been recorded ramming calves to death, nose-first, like football players.

Over forty species of primates kill their own young. Our ancestors? Darwin doubted they participated in such barbarity: they weren't that "perverted," he wrote. Goodall observed female chimps killing and eating baby chimps.

Thirty percent of infant deaths among certain baboons are the result of infanticide.

Postpartum depression will cause a human mother to murder her child. But scientists have said that most human infanticide is caused by social or economic woe. The mothers are almost always very young. If there's a choice between children, a boy and a girl? The girl goes.

An Aborigine tribe has been documented killing a child to feed it to another. In the New Guinea Highlands, mothers kill their daughters and then try again for sons. !Kung mothers will walk into the forest with an unwell newborn and then walk back alone.

There is not a culture on earth in which a parent has not killed a child.

What was in Medora Slone's nature that day when she twisted a rope around the throat of her own boy in a root cellar? Look to the woods, he knew, not the books. The annals of human wisdom fall silent when faced with the feral in us.

On this motel bed at the rim of the world, Core could feel himself forgetting how to know, how to believe.

IV

Vernon Slone landed in Alaska after dark, not in uniform but in dungarees fitted around combat boots, a baseball cap without a logo, a wool parka from a dead man at the military hospital in Germany. A patch on his neck, another on his shoulder. His sandy mane gone long and a blondish beard of weeks, lips hidden by mustache.

He'd been days in Germany, or a week, he couldn't know for sure—the pills, blue and pink. Surgery to remove the lead in his shoulder and neck, some of it lodged in bone. Then the unclear flight to a base back home. Kentucky, he was told. News about his boy. News about his wife.

An Army doctor spoke at him. *No one contacted you? Someone was supposed to contact you.* Slone couldn't bring his face into focus; his voice came as if from underwater. *It's been two weeks—* He looked at papers in a folder. *It's been nearly two weeks. You should have been told this.*

A shock wave softened by science, by more blue and pink. Another distorted voice from underwater. A woman this time, in civilian clothes. A counselor. Gold crucifix nestled in her jugular notch. She sat in a chair opposite him, at a table in his room, by a window. Her individual words were English, he knew, but her sentences seemed something else altogether. She kept asking if he wanted to pray. Slumped in a chair, Slone looked out the window at the uniforms passing on the walkway. In another minute he was asleep with his forehead on the table.

Pulse felt everywhere in his body, in ears clotted with blood or clogged shut with cotton. Mention of a Purple Heart by a pock-faced officer he'd never seen before. Mention of a ceremony to honor him. Still more pills and the weighted sleep of the sick. He fell into some netherland of shade and vapor where faces are more creature than person, blurred screams stretched across silence. His son's name in his mouth.

In the sun outside. Someone pushed him in a wheelchair, though there was nothing wrong with his legs and the pain in his shoulder and neck had gone. A redheaded teenager dressed as a candy striper handed him a bundle of yellow roses, still in green cellophane—her breasts too large for her age, a face splattered with freckles, a mouth grotesque with metal, braces refracting sunlight that stung his eyes. She spoke a tongue he didn't know and nobody explained. He needed to weep but could not find the strength to do it.

Beams of sunlight segmented the room in cryptic patterns, from windows both west and east, it seemed. He could not understand this abeyance of order. Shadows from branches and twigs brushed the wall like bone arms. At evening the lamplight covered the corners in malign misshapes he tried to decode but could not. His son spoke to him in dreams and when he woke he found he'd been sobbing as he slept.

The waking world had an awkward way with time now. Alaskans, he'd been told, had the skewed circadian rhythm of arctic things, tuned in to a half year of dark and ice. In those nebulous corridors between wake and sleep he saw his father, that chapped man, skin like shale, fractured by tobacco and cold. Each time he woke he remembered the facts anew.

Days ago someone had given him printed pages of the news article, black-and-white photos of Medora and Bailey. Photos that were three years old, he saw, partial and faded from the printer's low ink. Only the top halves of the sentences were visible, so that it seemed as if they were only half true—seemed as if he himself might be in charge of making those sentences whole, of completing the details of this story.

By the time he boarded the plane home he had flushed the blue and pink pills. He was beginning now to emerge from that gauzy lair.

His boyhood companion Cheeon met him at the gate. Slone saw him there among the colorful others eager to greet family—six feet tall, half Yup'ik, a fixed expression of grief and resolve. He recognized his drab winter clothes, his boots, the strong tobacco scent of him. Black hair pouring from beneath a camouflaged hunter's cap. His five-year-old daughter was the second child taken from the village by wolves, but he said nothing of this to Slone.

The men did not speak a word, did not clasp hands or embrace, only met each other's eyes and nodded. Cheeon took Slone's duffel bag, then handed him a cigarette and Zippo, a bowie knife in a black leather sheath. Slone moved briskly through the airport with Cheeon beside him keeping pace. Once through the double doors he lit the cigarette, fit the knife into his belt at the small of his back, and looked to Cheeon, who nodded the way to the truck across the road in the parking deck.

The temperature was two degrees now and would drop toward twenty below by dawn. His visible breath and the sharp scent of winter—Vernon Slone knew he was home.

For the eighty minutes it took them to arrive at the town's morgue the men did not speak. Cheeon drove and smoked and smoked again, his window cracked an inch for vent. The raised white scar jutting from the corner of his mouth told of the autumn morning when fishing on the lake in the valley. Fourteen years old, Slone cast his lure, not looking, and hooked him clean through the mouth. A quick yelp and Cheeon grabbed for the line so Slone wouldn't cast. Slone snipped off the barb with side cutters and threaded out the hook, holding down his laughter as the blood leaked onto their boots and Cheeon cursed him with his eyes and teeth.

This reticence between them, both instinct and ritual, was a lifetime old. Squalling babes the same age, they'd become instantly quiet when brought together, each a balm for the other in some way no one could explain. Bow-hunting elk or deer from adjacent stands in spruce, they'd pass twelve hours in uncut quiet, hand signals between them a superior tongue.

The winter hunt required an uncommon silence when the cold killed the sounds of summer, when ice muffled the earth and caribou a mile off could hear a man move through snow. They passed whole weekends of fishing for king salmon and trout without a single sentence on the river for fear that the fish could hear. All through November nights in their tent they wrapped around one another for warmth and never thought to wonder about an affection this natural.

On the rubber floor mats of Cheeon's truck: a hammer, a crushed coffee cup, a torn-open box of condoms, cigarette filters fallen from the ashtray, .22 rounds that rolled when the truck turned. His head back against the seat, Slone looked at the roads he knew so well, and as they approached town he searched for changes in storefront windows, in street signs, in front yards, every few minutes sipping from a water bottle Cheeon had handed him. A mother walking along a shoveled sidewalk with her boy—Slone sat quickly forward, turned his head to look at them as they passed. Electricity was everywhere outside the truck window tonight—the illumination of lives. Slone thought about protons, electrons, electrocution.

* * *

They were met in the dim hallway of the town morgue by two detectives, a lab-coated coroner, and by Russell Core, the wolf writer who had discovered his boy two weeks earlier, the one who had last seen Medora Slone. Core and the detectives tried to offer handshakes, attempt a feeble form of condolence, but Cheeon raised a finger to his lips, shook his head for them to remain quiet, to keep back, and he unlatched the steel door to the coldroom for Slone to enter.

He entered alone. He saw his son in an extended corpse drawer, the sheet folded to his waist, toe tag nearly the size of the boy's whole foot and attached like a price. His cobalt boy had grown in the year he was gone, the boy's face bones altered from either time or death. Hair longer than he'd ever seen it. Burgundy stain beneath the paper skin of his throat. Dark bulbs beneath slitted lids. He looked unfed and Slone wondered if this was a trick of death.

He breathed through sobs as a woman breathes through birth—solar plexus sobs, and he gave in to them, knowing this was his only time, his only chance for tears. He let them come and pass. For long minutes they rippled over him. Then he placed his palm on the boy's pale chest, his birdlike ribs. He bent—his skull tight from weeping, a pressure through his neck and face. He touched his lips to the boy's and whispered, "Remember me."

* * *

In the break room at the morgue, dense with the scent of coffee, the detectives sat in craters on the sofa. Across from them Slone and Cheeon smoked at a table. Russell Core sat in an armchair to their left, staring into his cup. Donald Marium had asked him here; he said Core was the only link to what had happened in the village. On the wall in this room a painting of a moose in scarlet wig and lipstick. When they'd first entered, Cheeon considered this picture closely, as if it were a calculus equation.

The cop with the mustache said, "Do you have any idea where on earth that wife might've fled to, Vern? Any idea at all where she went to?"

"We'll get her," the fat one said. "She'll pay for it, Vernon. We've got leads, a few of them." He held a file folder, a sheaf of documents on Medora Slone: photos and maps and Slone could not guess what else.

The other with the mustache said, "We got her picture out all over the state. All over, Vern. Troopers looking high and low for the wife's truck. But it'd be real good if you could give us some idea of where that woman might've fled to. Into Canada, maybe? We been in touch with the Mounties there. Dumb asses, all of 'em, but we been in touch."

This cop drank from a miniature Styrofoam cup and seemed irked by the morgue's coffee. "I know it's a damn hard time for you, Vern, what that woman did."

Most of the people in this town weren't from here—they were

willful refugees from the lower forty-eight. Slone and Cheeon both could instantly spot a forty-eighter. The fat one, Slone guessed, was northern California, maybe Oregon. The mustached one was most likely from Texas. Migrated here to dabble in policelike work when not cutting down moose out of season. This wolf man was a midwesterner. They felt needed now, Slone guessed. Important. Useful in this dark.

Slone's left eyelid twitched as it often did when he went without sleep. He'd tried to nap on the plane but could not. He smashed out his cigarette and turned to see Core, his white wolf face and regal beard. He was sitting oppressed and silent in the armchair.

"You found my boy?" Slone said.

Core met his eyes, nodded yes, and glanced away. Slone half nodded in return, in his gratitude, his version of thanks said with the face. Core looked down at his feet, at the salt-stained boots that belonged to Vernon Slone, the boots Medora had let him borrow two weeks ago when he arrived. When Core realized he was wearing them his head lightened with embarrassment and he tried to cover one boot with the other but knew it was useless.

"Mr. Core was called here by your wife," the fat cop said. "Damn woman told him a wolf took your boy. Can you imagine that, such a thing?"

At twelve Slone had shot dead a wolf in the hills above Keelut. For a live target to practice on, for fear and for fun. When his father found out, he took Slone's rifle and slapped the spittle from the boy's mouth. He could recall the old man's sandpapered palm on the skin of his cheek.

Then his father gave him a just-born husky to care for, "to fix that hardness in you," he said. And Slone cared for the animal for a decade until it lost vigor and grew lumps. At his father's demand

Slone put it down himself with the .22 rifle, then buried it in the hills of Keelut beside the ravine. He felt certain—he was twenty—that he'd not again in this life undergo such gutting grief. He saw the dog everywhere, smelled it on clothing, heard it in the cabin, dreamed of it. Haunted and bereft, he learned then, were an unforgiving pair.

The mustached one said, "We thought you'd have some questions for Mr. Core, Vern, since he was there, since he saw that woman last. He's been a help to us so far."

Slone turned again to Core in the armchair, sipped from his own coffee. He examined his knuckles, his wedding band, and under a thumbnail a blood blister that puzzled him. Each finger seemed a marvel of movement.

"Can you raise the dead?" he asked finally.

"No, sir, I cannot," Core said.

"Then I've got no questions for you."

"I'd like a cigarette, please," Core said.

Slone looked. He did not understand.

"Can I get a cigarette from you?" Core asked again.

Slone passed the pack to him then, and Core, nodding thanks, fingered one free from the box—the same unknown brand Medora had shared with him when he first arrived in Keelut, a black dagger for a logo. He reclined again and lit it from Slone's lighter and sat staring at its glow.

"You can't think of where the wife's gone to, Vernon? Anywhere at all?" the fat one asked. "A relative or friend, maybe? That woman have friends, any friends at all?"

Slone rose from the table then, bored by this, and Cheeon followed. Core stayed seated with the cigarette, his body still aching and warm from a flu that would not leave. The fizzing medicine he'd drunk an hour earlier had done nothing to quell the fever.

The detectives stood. The fat one said, "We need a statement when you could, Vernon, and a bunch of damn papers that need signing. At the station would be best, if you're all set to go. Don Marium is there, you know Don? He asked us to meet you here and then bring you over to the station, if you wouldn't mind it. Sooner would be better than later, most likely."

Slone stared at the cop and said nothing.

"Shit, we know you just got back, Vern. We're sorry as shit about all this. The more time we wait, the farther that woman gets, is what I'd say. We got them leads, a few we wanna go over with you, if you don't mind coming on back now. I know it's late. We got a map set up on the board there."

Cheeon stood before the painting, once again inspecting the moose in wig and lipstick, somebody's idea of a gag in a morgue, this abomination he could not comprehend. When Russell Core began snoring in the armchair all four men turned to look at him.

* * *

In the lampless parking lot behind the morgue, Slone and Cheeon stood at the detectives' truck and watched the wolf man drive off into whatever night awaited him, whatever fate was ready to claim him. His headlights showed sideswept flurries that by first light would thicken into a scrim of snow.

They turned to piss shoulder to shoulder in the plowed berms at the edge of the dark lot, streams of yellow slapping into hardened snow. Slone could see the white and orange lights of town, the blinking red eye of the radio tower beyond the rails.

The fat one spoke behind them. "You boys wanna follow us on over? We have coffee waiting there, good coffee, warm you right up. Put a splash of bourbon in there and you're all set."

Slone zipped his fly and took the .45 from Cheeon in the dark. He turned and shot the fat one through the face from a yard away.

He shot the other through his forehead.

They dropped near their car and Slone stood above them and shot each again through his earhole, then braced the handgun in his belt. Cheeon passed him a flashlight and Slone saw fragments of skull and brain stuck frozen to the side door of their car. He bent with the light to gather the fallen papers on Medora—a black-and-white photo of her face drizzled with blood and specked wet with snow—and slipped them back into the file folder. He looked again at the bodies, hardened blood like rubies scattered across a canvas of white.

Cheeon took the flashlight and folder from him and started the truck. Slone reentered the morgue through its rear loading door—inside an unlit hallway and the red glow of an exit sign. Minutes later he emerged with a body bag in his arms like a bride. At the back of the pickup, tailgate lowered, Cheeon held one end of the boy. They set him lovingly into the bed of the truck, where he sank several inches into a one-foot pad of snow.

An hour's drive to Keelut and the men did not speak. Cheeon smoked and drove as Slone reclined, his head turned to the bleached world he knew: houses, cabins, buildings, outside of town the numberless acres of land, not even the pledge of light in miles of such sable stillness.

The memory of alien sand, that slamming sun, the sheer exhaustion of those memories. Slone slept, the truck's tires a lullaby on asphalt.

* * *

Those first days towns or sectors of the city were always in smolder. Planes gave ruin. After, teams wheeled in block by block to find what still had breath. They crept door to door while buildings burned, smoke like night that made moon of sun. The men they sought seemed never to be where they should. Most were not in uniform. It was hard to know who should be shot, who would shoot. Families huddled in basements. Street dogs deafened and concussed, their ribs hunger-sharp. Gunfire on the next block, east or north, impossible to know.

Slone turned and found himself separated. Ducked into a doorway, squatted there for air. He swilled from a canteen, wiped sweat and filth from his brow. Voices, American, in a rubble-packed alley. Smoke like walls in the street.

When he stood in that entranceway he saw into the glassless window, through one rounded room into another: a soldier with a scalp of honey down, wearing Slone's own colors, his flag, from his company or not—his eyes still burned from sweat and smoke. A girl beneath this man's weight on a table, her bottom garb twisted aside. Slone watched him, a tattooed piston between her legs.

He entered the house with a voyeur's crawl. And he watched. The girl was very young, he saw now, sixteen or seventeen. Umber skin aglint with both her sweat and his. She did not struggle. She did not yell. She could not look away. She studied the soldier's face as if needing to remember it for some future use. Or else stunned by this adder, astonished that this shaitan could have honey-colored hair and such straight teeth. But for the quiet drip of tears she seemed almost partner to this.

More gunfire on the street. Rapid explosions nearby that sent a tremor through the floor of this house. The hissing of steam he could not guess the source of.

And then Slone was behind them. He saw nonsense hieroglyphs etched into the soldier's biceps. A medieval cross inked into his nape, and inside the cross a question: *Why hast thou forsaken me?*

He unsheathed the knife from his belt. The hand, the forearm, the shoulder—they can know their aim independent of mind. He stabbed this soldier through the right ear. A centimeter of the knife's tip poked through his left temple and Slone felt the body go limp on the blade. He held the man's drooped form upright with the knife so he would not topple onto the girl. He then thrust him quickly back and yanked free the blade in the same even motion. The serrated side of the knife was crammed now with bone and brain. On the dusty stone floor the man's blood puddled about his head more in black than red. His tattoo's useless question died with him.

Why has he forsaken you? Ask him yourself.

The girl sat up, leaking blood from her center. She covered her bottom half, crossed her legs on the table, wide-eyed at Slone not two feet from her. The bleeding blade still tight in his grip. He hadn't thought light-colored eyes a possibility among these people, but the girl regarded him now with a teal astonishment. Unsure what else that blade would thirst for. Unsure if another yellow-haired man would pry into her now too.

I can't hurt you, he thought. *I won't. Do not fear me.* And she seemed able to read these thoughts, to find in his face something she could not find in the other's. She did not tremble or flee—her tears had abated—and she could not look away from him. On the inner thigh of his pants Slone wiped the matter from the blade and held out the knife hilt first.

She was ready to read his expression: *Use this next time. Kill any man, any person who tries to bring you harm.* And she took the knife from him then. This gift. For a reason known only to her, she brought it to her nose to sniff its metal and hilt. She stood from the table and tucked the knife into her unclean garb. She looked to the body at her feet and spat onto it. She reached for Slone's right hand, tarry with the soldier's blood, and turned it over to inspect his palm. With her index finger she traced an invisible letter or sign no one but she would ever know.

Then she limped barefoot from the rear of the house and disappeared into roving smoke.

* * *

Russell Core's motel room smelled of two weeks of sickness, a DO NOT DISTURB tag warning away eager maids from the doorknob. Take-out food plastic from the one Chinese restaurant in town. Damp towels over chairs, a bed disrupted. Newspapers fallen on a floor more concrete than carpet, crinkled bottles of springwater in the trash. Torn packages of flu medicine, balled tissues, mugs of tea for the burn in his throat. On the dresser a chipped ceramic figure of a grinning Hawaiian girl in grass skirt and lei—Core could not decide if this was a joke or not.

For three days after the hunt his legs and back had ached, painful even to step to the toilet—an insistent reminder of his unfitness and age. His sleep was long and hazy with sickness. He'd wake not knowing the day, fight to recall which month this was. After several minutes not moving he'd remember: the dead boy, Medora Slone, his own wife no longer herself. A daughter he needed to see.

Since finding the boy he'd waited for two weeks for the return of Vernon Slone. He waited for a call that would finally tell of his wife's death. But no one knew where he was. He slept away those shortened days, mildly frightened of a sky that gray, of whatever impulse had led him to this place.

Back from the morgue now, he understood that he had waited for nothing. His daughter's phone number and address were folded in his wallet like a invitation sent to the wrong man. There was nothing Vernon Slone wanted from him, not another fact he could feed this family's horror.

And if Slone had asked him for an explanation? Would he have accepted the facts Core had to tell, the facts he knew of the wild? Those facts he had learned were no help here—no help to Slone and no help to himself. Awake in the night, the memory of Medora Slone's scent strong in him, he studied starlight from the window. What Medora had done was observable in nature. He'd seen it himself among starved wolves in the north. It was a fact he knew. But a fact that could do nothing to describe this.

The stale motel room around him, and the end or start of something else now, a new direction he couldn't gauge. Core unlatched the window, an eight-paned iron relic he had thought long extinct, ferns of frost on its glass. He swung it open into the outer black to let the cold clean this room. He knelt before the dark, his tears consumed now by a chaotic beard. He attempted his prayer but the words would not come to him, so completely had he lost them, so surely was he numbered among the damned. He stayed there at the open window until the night's cold turned to novocaine, until he found exhaustion enough to sleep again.

* * *

Behind the hills of Keelut, Slone and Cheeon dug at the rear of a graveyard hidden in a clearing between two expanses of wood. A wolf keened from deep in the valley beyond, and from low branches of cedar, owls watched this midnight's work. They dug sideways into the embankment of snow with shovels and pickaxes, clearing a temporary tomb. Without equipment the ground was impossible to pierce now. Their labor was illuminated by the truck's headlights, snow swirling in the beams as if insects at a lamp in summer. The dark beyond seemed more than night, seemed a deliberate negation of day.

As boys they'd hunted here in autumn and winter, lynx and grouse, even though they'd been forbidden by their fathers to take game where the dead lay. Proper burial for the boy would have to wait till after breakup when the ground softened. For now Slone's son belonged in this ancient earth of the village with his forebears. The boy's grandfather, Slone's own father, was buried just yards from here, in a hole chiseled down into the earth by these same two men. All the graves and gravestones concealed now by drifts of new fall.

They swung the pickaxes into the bank of snow. Side by side they seemed railway workers who have absorbed each other's rhythm. They did not stop for water or smoke. Slone's neck and shoulder wounds ached with each swing. The boy lay on the snow in his bag, in hushed witness to his father's work.

Halfway through the thickest layer, Cheeon left the grave to Slone and went to the truck's bed to carpenter the boy's coffin. Three sheets of plywood, a handsaw and hammer, a tape measure and a score of tenpenny nails, pencil behind his ear, lantern perched on a toolbox giving some light. What he fashioned so quickly was just a box. But it was even and tight and all they could offer till they had more light and time, till the thaw came.

Slone stopped five feet into the bank. Out of the hole, he drank from the thermos Cheeon had taken from the cab and tossed to him.

They unzipped the boy from the bag and placed him in the box. Slone touched his face, turned away, and could not resist a second time. He then hammered on the lid, twenty-two nails. Over the coffin Cheeon grabbed for Slone's left arm, rolled the sleeves to the elbow, and slid a pocketknife blade diagonal across his forearm. He squeezed until globs of blood pooled like wax at the head of the box, then with a naked finger inscribed a glyph that looked part wolf, part raven—a symbol taught to him by his Yup'ik mother. Slone did not ask what the marking was meant to ward off or welcome, but trusted his boy was protected beneath it.

They carried and slid the box into the cubby they'd made, then took up shovels again to conceal what lay within.

* * *

His home, the cabin he'd built, was girdled in police tape. Slone stood at the front door and looked. The boy's sneakers by the portable heater, his tiny snow boots. Winter coat on a hook. The lightbulb above him blinked and dimmed. He stepped in, the bones of the cabin made taut by cold, by the absence of human warmth. They creaked beneath his feet. He clicked on the electric heater, pulled wood from under the tarp on the rear porch, stacked it thick and high in the hearth. Then he started kindling in the stove, blew the flame to life until he could no longer see his breath.

He stepped toward the sofa still in his coat. A whirling, a rocking on feet half numb. The black snap of the bulb above him. Then Slone was falling, asleep before he could feel the sofa catch his weight.

Awake before dawn, he poured boiling water on freeze-dried

coffee. He knew that at first light the dead men behind the morgue would be found, and then he'd have scant time before police arrived here for him. Three or four hours in this weather, five tops. He stood in the root cellar to see the hole where the wolf writer had found his boy. He moved near to touch it, to smell the cold of it.

A meal of old eggs and hardened bread—he tasted nothing—and at the table he opened the folder of documents on Medora. A police report in faded ink. Photographs of his boy on the floor of the cellar. Where the Chevy Blazer might have been seen. Map of the highway between cities and east toward Yukon, a single blacktop artery with paved and unpaved roads branching off like capillaries.

On the map red dots indicating a possible direction. Many roads, he saw, were not marked, were unknown to townsfolk and cops, most no more than paths trimmed through a hide of birch and alder, unseen from the air. Both he and Medora had been on those hidden paths since childhood, since they'd first learned to ride snow machines, four-wheelers, dirt bikes. Wherever she'd fled, she'd fled, he knew, on those paths. He lit the folder at a corner, blew on the flame till it rose, then dropped it in the hearth to burn.

Aspirin for the ache in his shoulder, then more coffee. He stood at his wife's bureau and turned over each sheet of paper, each envelope. Unwashed laundry in a wicker basket by his foot: he brought her socks and underthings to his nose and mouth and inhaled the dank scent of her. At the bottom of the basket was the boy's T-shirt, a red race car with a bumper face that smiled—it still held his child's smell. Slone slipped it into his jacket pocket. In the bedroom he emptied her dresser and stripped the bed. Beneath her pillow an Inuit shaman's mask made of driftwood and pelt—the face of a wolf.

He sat on his son's bed. He looked and looked more and did not blink. Outside, the morning moved without him.

He began filling duffel bags. Socks and gloves, thermal leggings and insulated overalls. A hunting knife, ammunition, clips, cartridges. Compound bow and quiver. Maglite and rope. Field glasses. From the bathroom: ibuprofen, antibiotics, aspirin, bandages, peroxide, razor blades, stool softener. In the hollow floor of the closet a compartment of firearms: 9mm handgun, twelve-gauge autoloader, Remington rifle that had belonged to his father. The AR-15 semiautomatic he found near the back door: what the wolf man had taken on his hunt.

Cheeon had disentombed his Bronco from snowfall, changed the battery and fluids, filled the tank, draped the engine with an electric blanket to warm it back from death. Into the back hatch Slone loaded the duffels and guns. Blankets, a pillow, two containers of gas, snow boots. Pickaxe, shovel, chain saw. A sack of nonperishables with peanut butter, crackers, chocolate. The truck turned over with the first crank of the key and Slone let the engine rev and warm, the windshield and rear defrosters droning on high. He loaded the pistol and tucked it into his belt, then the shotgun and placed it beneath the seat.

Then he made for the old woman.

* * *

The village's main road was vacant this soon after dawn. In the year he'd been gone nothing he could see had changed here. The men and boys had left already for hunting, or to check their lines in the holes they'd drilled at the lake. Women tended to children and chores inside their cabins. A team of sled dogs staked beside a home stood in silence when they saw him and lay down again as he passed. The old woman's hut sloped beside the generator shack.

It had been there since long before he was a boy, behind the well house—a place they'd all avoided as children.

When he entered she was upright in a chair at the mouth of the fire, rocking among distaff and debris, among cordwood, pelts, stacks of leather-bound books arrayed as furniture. In this single-room hut the heavy stench of wood smoke, of boiled moose, unwashed flesh. On the back wall an old wrinkled poster of a soccer player in mid-kick. No appliances, just that woodstove, a teakettle and pot on top of it. Slone closed out the mass of cold behind him and slid the serrated blade from his boot.

"Vernon Slone," she said. "You came home, Vernon." She looked to the blade in his hand. "You come now to punish the old witch. But I am no witch. I knew you'd come. You're home now, Vernon Slone."

He stepped toward her and considered her pleated neck, the fire's light in her eyes, her jowls in divots from some childhood scourge.

She pointed to a crate overturned at her stumped feet. "Sit," she said, and he did—he sat close enough to smell the filth of her.

"You think I could have saved the boy, me an old woman? You think I knew? I've known things since before your father's birth. But nothing I know has mattered. Go to your father's grave, ask him yourself. Ask the spirits. Take your wrath to the gods, to the wolves, not an old woman. Take it to yourself if you want to be rid of this, Vernon Slone."

In her hands a fabric doll, without nose or mouth—something meant to hex or help.

"It was foretold in the ice, that boy's fate. Hers as well, from the start. There was nothing an old woman could do. Punish yourself. The both of you. You left this place for war, Vernon Slone. You should have died there. There in the sand. That was your fate. You chose not to accept it. So this, this is what you come home to."

She shook the doll at him, then placed it on a mound of books beside her. Wood snapped in the hearth and the fire flared against the polish of Slone's blade. She pointed to a table near him. "My pills," she said, and he passed her the prescription bottle, medicine brought once a month by a doctor in town. Her hands trembled as she uncapped the bottle, as she placed a pill on her tongue and swallowed without water.

"This wasn't the first time the wolves came to Keelut. The elders here remember it as I do. We were children. What came before the wolves, the white man called it Spanish flu. We called it *peelak*. Half this village died in it. Half, I tell you. The sickness got the brain, the lungs, the belly. No one has told you this history, Vernon Slone, your own history here?"

He sat and said nothing.

"It was winter and some, like my father, those who held memories from the coast, they made snow igloos behind the hill. We kept the bodies there, protected there. A hundred bodies. Two hundred. No one would come here to help us. No one would dare come here to help. Each morning we'd wake to new death in the huts of this village. People drowned. Drowned in their own fluid. Their lungs filled with the sickness. Or their brains burned from the fever. They leaked from the bowels. They leaked day and night and were too weak to move."

She leaned forward in the rocker.

"We could smell them. My father told me to stay away but I could see, see him carry a man, almost dead, this man, carry him to a sled. Pull the sled around the hill to the snow igloos they made there. This man I saw wasn't dead. He looked at me shivering, his eyes very alive. My father and others, they stacked him in the igloo with the dead. He died there very soon. He died there with the dead, moaning in the cold with the dead. I could hear him over the hill."

When she motioned for the jug of water on the floor, Slone passed it to her handle-first.

"The moans in the night were very bad. We stayed awake in bed listening, my sister and me, cuddled in the same bed, we listened. The blanket over our heads to keep the sickness out. And we listened, we did. Once when my father was trying to save a woman, he sent my sister and me, sent us to the creek to cut the ice for water. We hurried to do this. In dark and cold we hurried and chopped the ice for him. You know what we heard?"

Slone watched her face, the pencil-thin and chapped pale lips folded in on themselves.

"We heard them howling. Howling beyond the valley that night. We hurried and melted ice for my father as he told us. He stayed with this woman. He stayed until morning, giving her the water. He told us the water would save her. If she kept drinking it would save her. But she slept finally at the dawn and didn't wake. She never woke. My father stacked her on the dogsled with the other dead and brought them to the igloos behind the hill."

Slone, still intent on the old woman's face, passed the blade slowly back and forth in callused hands.

"The next morning my father and others found what happened in the snow igloos. The wolves got in, they tore apart the bodies of the dead in the night. They feasted in gore on those many corpses, a hundred bodies. Their frozen blood and bones were all over the hillside, strewn. Scattered everywhere. Not a single body was spared by the animals. From the tracks my father saw the size of this pack. Over twenty wolves had come, had feasted that night. It seemed a fate worse than the influenza. Everybody then gathered the bones, all the bones they could find, gathered them in baskets for proper burial when breakup came. But there is no proper burial after such a thing."

She took up the doll again and caressed its head as if it had life.

"That is the history here, our history, Vernon Slone. You cannot blame an old woman for that."

Minutes later, his wrist and hand gluey with the old woman's blood, Slone walked back into the brimming day. He stood breathing in the cold. If the villagers knew he was back they did not come from their cabins, neither to welcome nor damn him. Across the road he saw curtains part and close. He returned to his truck and looked over his home a final time.

Then he was gone from that place, fled down icy passageways that could not be called roads—paths through a wilderness forged long before his birth.

V

At this December dawn behind the town morgue Donald Marium saw ice crystals shine atop the newest snowfall, drifts rolling to a dun-hued horizon. He took in the men's faces as they gazed upon the killed—shot dead, they lay frozen and twisted by the wheel of their truck. Snow had been dusted from their corpses to reveal splashes, rivulets of glassy blood. Across the open compass behind town, north toward the range, he saw snow-burdened trees bowed like penitents. The morning seemed made of muslin, the sun less than a smudge. The wind came in soughs and shook free a pine scent from trees, then sent snow aloft as mist.

Every one of these cops had seen deer and caribou and wolves like this, marten and muskrat, Dall sheep turned from white to red. A few had witnessed men dead of cold and wet in swollen rivers, or of long plunges from headwalls. Some had tried to rescue children yanked underwater, lost beneath capsized canoes, yoked to the bottom. But Marium understood that most here had never witnessed fellow men like this. He himself had seen such a mess only once before, and not in this town.

He spoke to the cop standing behind him. "What's in the building?"

"Another one dead. Frank the coroner, we think."

"You think?"

"Shit, Don, we can't get near enough him to see. He's in a whole lake of blood, in his office."

"Dead how?"

"Dead all the way through, it looks to me."

"You find the casings here?" he asked.

"The what?"

"Shell casings. How do you think these men were killed? With some tickling? Dig up that spot for the casings, please."

"How do you know it's this spot?"

"Those wounds are nearly point-blank. You see the faint star pattern of that wound? On that man's face there? You're standing on the shell casings."

"Something from here did this?"

"I'd say a someone did it. Dig up the casings, please."

"Feels like a something to me. First that village kid, and now this. What a goddamn shitty way to end the year. That kid's gone, you know."

"Gone how?"

"His body, it's gone. They took the kid's body. You ever see anything like this?"

"Not quite like this, no. Please find the casings."

Marium stood smoking a cigarette in the cold as men continued this work. The ambulance sat silent and without use, its lights pointlessly in twirl. His dreams in the night had offered him no sign of what this day held.

The morgue's waxed hallways squeaked beneath a racket of wet boots. A half-moon of cops stood at the cusp of the coroner's blood. He lay facedown and Marium could see the stab wound was in the side of his head, through the ear and out the other side.

"You boys waiting for Frank to sit up and tell you who did it? Mop right up to him, please, and look for boot marks as you go."

"What about forensics, Don?"

"About what?"

"The guys from the city."

"You photograph this room?"

"Took a hundred shots."

"Then you and a mop are as forensic as it'll get right now. Look for a goddamn boot mark, please, and stop if you see it."

"I thought the city guys were coming. Or troopers, something. How in the hell we supposed to handle this?"

Marium smiled at him. "Troopers. That's a good one. I didn't realize troopers even knew we were here, this town. Let's think of this as our own mess for now. Stop touching things, please."

His salmon-and-eggs breakfast sat half eaten on his kitchen table. He thought of coffee, Susan, his wife, in her bathrobe and nothing underneath, toenails the pink he liked. Twelve years younger, redheaded and lithe, she was a former dancer of ballet. Her breath stayed sweet even at waking. She was his promise of thaw in this place. She wanted children and kept Marium engaged in the task, early-hours coupling with an erotic unclean scent on her. He was prepared for kids, willing now at forty-eight.

At the rear of the hall he stepped into the break room. He could smell the cigarette smoke stuck on curtains and patted a jacket pocket for his own pack. He saw dents in the sofa cushions where heavy men had sat. Other rooms, offices down a second hallway, and the metallic coldroom at the end. He'd been to this morgue dozens of times over the years—to sign papers for old people dead from sickness, or young people dead from being dumb—but he'd never entered this coldroom. Never wanted to.

He grabbed the handle with a latex glove, pulled to open the door, then entered in the kind of caution born of superstition. The extended corpse drawer was empty, the sheet thrown aside. On the floor beneath it lay a toe tag in blue ink. He crouched to get it and read the name, read the numbers telling all of Bailey Slone.

Looks like your daddy's home, boy.

* * *

Cheeon answered the knock, opened his front door and kept it open, a cigarette glowing to its stub, the heat from a cast-iron stove pushing at the cold. Marium's coat was unzipped to show no weapon in his underarm holster. When he saw Cheeon's cigarette he retrieved one of his own from a coat pocket. The men leaned against the doorframe smoking, looking fifty yards out in front of Cheeon's two-level cabin where police vehicles sat arranged on the snow front to back, four of them. The men behind wore flak jackets and helmets, their rifles lowered, some sipping from cups of coffee hastily got.

"Was wondering when you'd show up here."

"I told them I'd try talking to you, Cheeon. See if I could get you to come without any goddamn mess here. I'm not claiming to be a friend. I wouldn't claim that."

"If you say."

"But we've talked over the years, when you were in town. Had coffee a few times, if memory serves. We've been friendly, anyway. Our fathers knew each other, I think. Your wife and girl were friendly with me. With Susan too, my wife. Would you agree with that?"

"If you say."

"And that has to mean something."

Cheeon spat, half in the snow, half on his boot.

"If you say. But I don't think it means what you want it to mean right now, guy. Not even close."

A scud of wind lifted loose snow from roofs and moved across open space in a white swirl. The late morning sun was just a peach smear.

"I'm from this place just like you."

"You ain't from this village."

"No, not from here, but not that far from here."

"You come to tell me your life story, guy?"

"We've got two cops killed out back of the morgue in town, Cheeon. Also the coroner inside with a knife wound through his head. And then there's a missing dead boy. That's what we've got here, Cheeon."

He nodded and smoked but did not look at Marium.

"You list those dead in order of importance? Because a couple of dead cops is cause for a party around here."

"No, I did not. I'm not saying that dead cops are something special, more special than anyone else dead. Dead all around is not a good thing, you ask me."

"I can think of some sons of bitches that might do the world a bunch of good dead."

"That's fine. I ain't disagreeing. I just don't want anyone else dying here today if we could help it, please."

"Looks like you came expecting it, though. All these cops out here."

"Like I said, I told them I'd try talking to you first. See if we could prevent a mess here."

"Come quietly, you mean. That's the cop phrase, right? Come quietly."

More silence while they smoked.

"Cheeon, most of these cops out here aren't our redneck guys from town. They're Feds, city boys, and they've got a fair amount of firepower they're ready to use today."

"I've got a fair amount of my own I'm ready to use."

"I know it. That's why we're talking here, Cheeon. Your father was busted a few times for illegal firearms. You know what they say about that apple not falling far."

"Nope. I don't know nothing about that apple. But it'd be real smart of you, guy, not to mention my father again."

"Okay. I won't. It was either you or Slone who killed those men and took that child. Maybe it was the both of you. I know you boys have been tight since way back."

"Vernon's gone to the desert. There's a war there. You got a radio?"

"Vernon Slone is home. You know that. And you helped him. I was just at his cabin. Looks like I missed him by five or six hours."

"If you say."

"Listen, Cheeon. Whatever happened, we've got to get it figured. The cops were shot with a .45 Springfield. You've got one of those registered."

"I've got others not registered."

"I figured that. Frank, the coroner, was retiring this year, moving to San Diego, I believe. Hell, he wasn't even a real coroner. Just a doctor who did the job for us because no one else could do it."

"San Diego, huh? Never heard of it."

"He was stabbed straight through his head. Clear through, from one side to the other. Who'd do a thing like that?"

"You tell me."

"You can probably guess he had some family who won't be the same."

Cheeon nodded more, smoked more, nearly smiled. His fingernails were piss-tinted from tobacco.

"Yeah," he said. "There's a bunch of that going around here lately."

"Where is Vernon Slone, Cheeon?"

Cheeon turned to him, smoke funneling from his nostrils. His face—a crimped brow, the start of a smirk—said, *You're dumber than you look if you think I'll tell you that.*

"Yeah, okay," Marium said. "Maybe you'll tell me where that boy's body is, then. It's state evidence."

"It's what?"

"Evidence."

"That boy's body is nothing to you and your like. It's not of this earth anymore. Put that boy out of your mind or he just might haunt you, guy."

"Where's Medora Slone?"

"She'll be found. Not by you or them, though."

"What happened to her? How does that happen to a woman?"

"How in the goddamn hell should I know? I ain't a woman."

A span of silence now. Cheeon pressed out the filter into ice with a boot toe, then lit another.

"What's the temp today?" he asked. "Feels like a February cold is coming on and it ain't even January yet."

Marium pointed. "Thermometer says zero right there."

Cheeon looked at the thermometer screwed into the outside sill of the kitchen window.

"That's broken. It's been stuck on zero all year, even last summer." He stopped to pull in the smoke. "Maybe it's not broken. I don't know."

"Is that why those cops were shot?" Marium said. "So no one but Slone would find Medora? So no one would interfere in his business? His revenge, whatever he wants. And Frank because the big galoot just got in the way?"

"What do I look like, like I enjoy all these fucking questions from you, guy?"

"I know your little girl was taken from here by a wolf. I know you don't have a body to bury and that there's nothing on earth worse than that."

"You know that, huh? A lot of help you were for a guy who knows that. You come an hour across the goddamn snow for my sorry ass but you wouldn't come for some kids dead in the hills."

"We came."

"You came and you left and you didn't come back. Worthless as shit, you city boys. Though even shit can fertilize, right? What can you do?"

"We ain't city boys, Cheeon, you know that."

"You sure as hell are. I've been going there my whole life, I know what the goddamn city is."

"We're an hour closer to Anchorage than you. That don't make us the city. Five thousand people is hardly a city, I'd say."

Cheeon bent with laughter, coughed on his smoke. Laughed more, his teeth as stained as his fingers.

"You come here today to argue with me about the definition of a city, guy? You must have goddamn nothing else in the whole world to do."

"I'm not arguing, Cheeon. No one's arguing. I'm just talking. And I'm saying: we're not that different from all of you here."

"That's where you're wrong. That's one of the places you're wrong. You went to college and you're dumber than dog shit."

"Okay, then. I'm wrong and dumb, I don't deny that. I'm just saying. We're not all bad. We helped get the plumbing set up in this village five or six years back. Helped put this place on the grid."

"And now you want a goddamn trophy for letting these people take a shit in their own house. Ain't you something."

"I don't want anything, Cheeon. I'm just saying."

They looked at each other then, held one another's eyes for half a minute until Marium glanced away. What he saw in Cheeon's face just then was more than a mingling of rage and grief. It was a fundamental otherness that frightened him.

"Some of these cabins are still dry."

"Some old-timers didn't want electric and plumbing. That's not our fault, Cheeon."

"Feels good when you say that, don't it? *It's not our fault.* You really are goddamn something."

"Okay. I know it's bad here right now. I'm not disagreeing with that."

"You know a lot of stuff, I gotta hand it to you. But it's way past bad. There a word for way past bad? You learn that word in college?"

"There might be one for let's not make it worse. You've got a wife who probably needs you, I'd say."

"She's gone from here."

"She'll be back. It's her home, ain't it?"

"She won't be back. No one wants to come back to what happened here. This village will be a ghost town in a year, just watch."

More quiet, a cigarette lighter shared, more smoke between them, thick white in the cold.

"I'm sorry for all this, Cheeon. I really am."

"I've been thinking about it. Them dead sons of bitches at the morgue? Bastards like you and me? When we're killed the past is killed, and the past is dead already, so no big deal. But when kids are killed? That's different. When kids are killed the future dies, and there ain't no life without a future. Is there?"

"We have futures."

A look now, more smirk than smile. "You're wrong again there, guy. Our futures end today. The raven follows the wolf, and the wolf has come for you and me. Look there." He pointed to a snowed-in spruce, a raven in a branch like an ink blotch with eyes.

"You can blame starved wolves for what happened to your little girl but you can't blame a person."

"You can always blame a person. The world ain't nothing but persons, every goddamn one of them starved for something."

From behind the bulwark of vehicles police spied through field glasses. One on a satellite phone. A sniper in white camouflage on the ground beneath hanging slats of snow-heavy pine. Minutes more of quiet and smoke.

"Those boys look like they're not sure whether to shit or piss."

"I won't lie to you, Cheeon. Most haven't taken part in anything like this before, not that I know of anyway. But that's bad for you, not good. Because when you're scared you're stupid. And stupid doesn't go too well with guns."

"I'd bet they're stupid no matter what. What'd you all expect? Me to walk on out with my hands in the air? Some shit like that?"

"I'm just trying to prevent as much stupidity as I can here. If you come with me today I'll make sure everything's fair. I'll assure you of that."

"Everything's what?"

"Everything's fair."

His laugh was a nasal sound caught between a chuckle and a snort. He looked at his cigarette to find it sucked down to the filter.

When he was a boy he told his father he'd grow to become a doctor. He could recall the doctors from town who came to Keelut when called, bright and hale, their forehead mirrors like coronets. He recalled the command, the godliness of them. At fourteen he was beset by the migraines of viral meningitis—some sickness from the white world. The doctor, a white man with the braided mane of an Indian, sank a tall syringe into his spine and pulled the milky fluid. He returned daily for a week to shoot him full of medication and nutrients, a liquid red B_{12} that made a body-wide inner burn and high.

"I ain't going with you, guy. You can forget that."

"It'll be a long dragged-out day, Cheeon. Into the night and morning, maybe. Phone call after phone call. Right now police are clearing these cabins behind yours, and those across the way there."

"Police can't clear these homes. These people won't move an inch for you sons of bitches."

"Well, we're trying. And there's police in the trees, and behind the house. I don't know about you, but I'm goddamn tired today, slept like shit last night. The wife had me up all hours trying for this baby she wants pretty bad. I'm not complaining of it, just saying."

"Well. I sleep like shit every night. Then sleep half the day gone."

"What about work?"

"Shit, there ain't been work. Every mine for fifty miles around is closing, you know that. We trawled the gulf for two straight weeks a while back and couldn't catch a goddamned halibut. Caught a sneaker."

"Things should improve."

"Hauled some cords of wood into town last month. Just once, though. There's a famine here. Some kind of famine I never heard of before."

"I never understood why you didn't join the service with Slone. You've done everything else together since birth."

"Do I look like someone who takes orders?"

"It's a paycheck."

"Do I look like a desert suits me? Because if you joined up these last ten years, you were going to the desert, guy."

"Slone didn't mind it."

"Well. Vernon's not like you or me. He has a . . . I don't know what to call it. A cunning on him. A way of making you think he's taking your orders when really he's doing exactly what he set out to do. But that takes a kind of cunning I don't got."

From inside his jacket pocket he took a flask and drank from it, then handed it over to Marium, who despite this morning hour drank too and passed it back to Cheeon.

"Where's your wife, Cheeon?"

"It don't matter. Not no more."

Marium lit another cigarette and shifted his body against the doorframe.

"I was on a raid one time, down in glacier country, outside Juneau. Before I came back up here for good, when my first marriage went to shit. A guy shot dead his wife in their hunting cabin. He wouldn't come out. A rich city fucker. Owned a company, cell phone towers, I think. After we were out there two straight days around the cabin he finally started shooting at us, shooting like crazy. We had to burn the place. We shot back for a while and then just burned it. Both of the bodies were nothing but charcoal stains when we went in."

"A rich fucker and his rich bitch wife, both of them dead. And the world is a better place."

"You know what bothered me the whole time? The goddamn boredom of it. Standing out there for two whole days. I can deal with bloodshed when I have to, but boredom I just can't stand."

"Don't worry," Cheeon said. "I'll give you the bloodshed long before the boredom."

Marium dropped the unfinished cigarette into the snow. He zipped his coat to the neck and stretched on gloves, then pulled the wool hat over ears flush from cold. "I'm sorry it has to be this way, Cheeon."

"I'm not."

"Think about what I offered you, please."

"And you think about that phone call your wife will get today. Imagine her there on the line when she hears it, hand on her belly. There's nothing on earth will stop that phone call now. You think about that, guy."

He walked back into the heat of his cabin, leaving the door unlatched behind him.

VI

Slone entered an old mining camp that had morphed into a shadow town without name, a commune pushpinned into the base of a bluff, mostly inaccessible by road. Beyond this place lay so many miles of tundra whole states could fit on its frozen breadth.

All the day before he had crawled through wilderness, on paths beneath canopies of cottonwood and birch that held most of the snow from recent fall. Only a six-inch pad of snow on these paths, but even in four-wheel drive with tire chains he had to crawl. He could tell that others from the village had recently crossed these trails: in trucks, on snow machines, on four-wheelers. Hours after nightfall he'd parked off the path and let the engine idle through the night for warmth. He ate from the food he'd taken from home, drank melted snow and wished he'd remembered to bring whiskey. Podded in a quilt across the back seat, he pressed his boy's T-shirt to his face and, inhaling its scent, he slept till light.

When he entered the mining camp the following day it was already near dark, the snow coming slantwise in sheets. The bluff above blocked the sinking sun and brought on early night. A memory stabbed at him then: he and his father here for a purpose he didn't know, nor could he know if the memory was even real. He left the truck between a bulldozer and a thousand-gallon fuel tank on four squat legs like a white rhino. In the onset dark, firelight began to burn in rude cabins and wood-frame buildings.

He walked along the unplowed center road, on snow waffled by truck tires. He saw snow machines in various states of dismantle, drays with wheels deformed by rust, truck tires in a heap. Empty pallets stacked for firewood. Lynx pelts splayed on racks, a pyramid of car batteries, sleds of birch, the well house to his right. Fifty-five-gallon drums everywhere, a slouched wanigan. Across the road a Quonset hut collapsed at its center, and beside it a full-sized school bus, its morning yellow gone beige, the windows shattered, gaping like kicked-out teeth.

He found a two-story inn with steel kerosene cans piled under the porch awning next to pole wood. Inside, an inky shadow spilled through rooms. With a fingernail he tapped the door's glass pane, then tapped again. The woman waved him in without turning to see what illness had just walked out of this winter night.

She was bent before a woodstove. "Very late in the season for travelers," she said, and turned then to look at Slone.

She wore men's snow boots and clothing of odd design, a project of marmot, caribou, and wolf. A storm of brittle hair to her waist, eyeglasses missing a lens. She jabbed into the flame with a brass poker. Halfway up the wall were drums of condensed milk, fifty-kilogram sacks of sugar, flour, rice, cans of apple butter and spinach in shrink-wrap. Against the opposite wall stacks of ammunition, .22- and .223-caliber, bird shot and buckshot. On a nail hung a model human skeleton from some school's anatomy class— it wore a red Santa's hat, a cigarette crammed between its teeth.

"I was here once," Slone said. "As a child."

The woman moved from the stove to the corkboard behind the front counter, a collage of photos tacked to it, most dulled sepia by the decades, some more recent with robust color.

"Well, then your picture might be here. We take every traveler's picture who comes through. What year was it, you say?"

"I was a kid here with my father. Why were we here?"

"He might've had a gold or silver claim. Most all of us came for that, unless you were scientists from the college or else hunters or trappers. Them scientists have been coming steady for the past decade, I'd say, on their way north. Every week there's something on the radio about glaciers melting and the world heating up. I told them scientists: last year it was fifty below and the year before that fifty-eight below and you can take my word, fellas, they feel the same in the lungs."

"That's my father," and he pointed into the mix of photos at a bearded man whose features told of neither place nor age, his eyes with no trace of the blue Slone recalled from youth. His father had long ago left off appearing in his dreams. He'd catch himself going weeks or months without remembering the man. Without wanting or needing to.

She removed the partially concealed photo from the board. "If this is your father, then this must be you here next to him. Handsome little fella."

She handed the photo to Slone. "That's probably twenty-five years ago," she said. "Judging from the film. They don't make that kind anymore, haven't for a while now, or at least I haven't been able to order any of it from the catalog. I miss that kind of film."

It had been so long since he'd looked upon his father's face, and upon his own as a child, that the somber pair in the photo seemed holograms, ghost-town twins of themselves. His stomach tore at the top. He could make out Bailey just barely in his own boyhood stare.

"I can keep this?"

"It's more yours than mine," she said. "I only click a button. Your face belongs to you, fella. It's a good-lookin' face."

"That one too?" He pointed to the newest photo, pinned to the far right corner of the corkboard.

"You know this one? She was just here. You missed her by a week and a half. She stayed a few nights. Strange thing is she shrieked a little when I took that picture. That was something new to me, I'd say. Who's she to you?"

"My family."

"That's an odd family traveling apart this far out, if I can say so. But you're welcome to the picture. I make duplicates. I was a photographer before I came into the country. Where're you in from?"

"Keelut."

"There's no road from there to here. Not directly."

"Not directly."

"Been here thirty years or more and I can say there's no easy road from there to here. My husband and me came up into this country from the lower forty-eight, to stake our claims. And here we still are. Most others are gone except for the twenty-odd of us. We like it, though. The others left for oil, when they were saying oil was the new silver and gold. Nothing quite matches precious metals, you ask me. We did mine this place bare, but it was good while it lasted, you bet."

"Why was she here?"

"No place else to be if you're in these parts, I suppose. She wanted to see our Indian hunter for some reason. We call him that, our Indian hunter, as a joke, you know, but he's just John, he's been around here forever. He's not a forty-eighter like the rest of us. He was raised on the Yukon, in a river tribe. He was here in this spot before a single miner showed up. And he's still here."

"Where'd she go?"

"Your girl there? Heck if I know. If she knew, she wasn't saying it to me. I like to talk, as you might imagine, living in the country, but she didn't want to hear any of it. This one stayed in the room, mostly. I cooked her food but she just stared out that window there, like she was waiting for something to come in and grab her. A pretty girl, too. But a bit odd, if I can say so, no offense. She had your same color hair. And nose, too, I think. Real pretty, but odd, like I say."

This photo in his fingers—her face just a week ago, a look of longing in it and something else not nameable, her irises all pupil. That green wool turtleneck was knitted by her two winters ago. She'd chopped her hair to her chin—it was waist-length when Slone had left. When he looked up he looked into the flashbulb of the woman's camera and it sent bolts through his eyes.

"You're a handsome fella," she said, trying to fix her hair. She rubbed lip balm across her mouth. Her lips were so thin they were barely there, eyebrow like an underline, whiskers in half sprout from her chin.

"Another storm's coming late tonight," she said. "Or else by morning, the radio says. You staying with us?"

Slone nodded, blinked the flashes from his eyes.

"I don't have any more bread, I have to warn you. Plane hasn't been back in two weeks. We're expecting Hank again any day now, if the storms slow. Last time he tried to land that ski plane in weather, he missed the runway and hit the bluff. We call it a runway, you know, but it's just a bulldozed road tamped down."

He looked again at the photo of Medora.

"Of course, there are some roads from the city to here, but you can't get a big enough truck along most of them, and anyway it takes more than a day. Plus you better know how to drive in snow because if you get stuck in a storm on one of those little roads you can forget being found till breakup. So we don't mind waiting for Hank and his plane. He takes supplies way beyond us even, where no roads go. Hank's a real good man, you bet."

"I want to stay in the same room she stayed in."

"There's only two rooms up there. You can have your choice, fella. No one's fighting over those rooms. Honestly, I haven't changed the sheets in there, if you don't mind it."

Slone stayed fixed on the photo and said nothing.

"Not sure what sort of battery you have in your vehicle but you might wanna pull it inside the garage there across the way. We call it the garage, you know, it's just a big corrugated metal hangar on a concrete slab. But there's a gas heater in there to keep the trucks from freezing up and it stays warm as the devil in fifty below. What're you driving?"

She bent to the window and with a sleeve wiped away the moisture to look out.

"That a Ford? Hard to see. I used to have a Ford, owned nothing but American, and then my husband said to me one day, he said, *We're not American anymore, we're Alaskan.* Last year after breakup he drove off to the city in the Ford and a week later drove back in a Jap model, a Nissan truck, or one of those SUV thingies. It's real roomy, better than the Ford, I have to say, what little I do drive of it."

"What's the room price?"

"Do you have any magazines?"

Slone stared.

"Magazines," she said. "No magazines? You didn't bring any with you to look at while you're traveling?"

"What magazines?"

"I'm not real picky about them," she said. "Any kind with pictures. I like them all. I usually just get paid in magazines."

* * *

Upstairs in the guest room—a compressed rectangle of wooded slats with the cold scent of stagnation—he looked in drawers, checked the closet, then beneath the bed. He peeled back the military-issue blanket and on his knees pressed his face into the sheet where Medora had slept. The vaguest outline of a fluid stain midway on the twin mattress—she slept nude no matter the month—and he thought he could smell her there. He breathed that way with his face to the sheet, then licked the stain.

He ignited the kerosene heater beneath the window, dimmed the lantern to a slow burn. Despite his hunger he stripped bare and reclined on the creaking bed as if his body could fit into the mold her own body had made. As if he could enter the morass of her dreams and learn her destination. He spent himself beneath the blanket, the first release in weeks, and fell asleep before he had the chance to clean his hand.

* * *

An ungodly night in some sere village east of the capital, the heat at ninety still, hours after the drape of dark. He'd been in the desert ten months and two days. A roundup of men now, shoulder to shoulder against the wall of a building chafed by sand and time. A score of bearded ghouls, hands zip-tied behind them, filthy bare feet, toenails like impacted corn. Molesting lights from the vehicles made their shadows on the wall as black as macadam.

Wet through with sweat and fighting to keep awake, Slone sat on a low porch step while others kept howling women at bay, ransacked more homes, guarded men at gunpoint. An inept translator spat gibber to these seized ones who shook their heads in ire and spat back. Shoddy rifles collected and stacked in a mound. Chickens in cluck on the road, a goat roped to a pole. Somewhere the skirl of an infant, and beyond the slap of spotlights a perplexing desert murk.

Now a chaos of conflicting reports, unabsorbed information. A corporal on the radio sucking on a clot of gum, getting no answer, none they wanted to hear. The man they sought was either among the seized or not, guilty or not. Eyes shut, Slone leaned back against the mud-brick wall of the house and sweated some more.

This undermanned platoon of twenty-two was from the start an errant brotherhood counting corpses and days. Half were drug and battery felons who'd been given waivers to enlist. They daily mocked those frayed others, those men in the news they heard so much about, men soothed by doctors in the States. Men who returned home cracked, only part of what they were before coming here. Ten months in now and Slone had not come close to the sunder, to the nightmares and the morning shakes. And he understood that he never would. That the eclipse in him had been there since his start. His was the nightly sleep of the exhausted sane.

His warped brethren could smell in Slone all he was capable of—a calmness masking an urge for carnage—and they feared him in a way they'd feared few before. His mere presence among these men seemed to turn them more lunatic, seemed to increase their will to ruin.

On the ground by his boot, partially hidden in rocks, lay a metallic object. A harmonica, nicked and dented. Slone blew bits of gravel from the air chambers and brought it to his lips. At the mounted .50-caliber gun behind the spotlight the gunner unloaded on the line of seized men, red-stained the wall behind them as they jolted from the impact, as women shrieked on soiled knees. Blood enough to course through dirt, holes in them to fit a fist.

Slone wanted to breathe a song into the harmonica but it made a clogged, rasping sound. He dropped it back into the yellow dirt and tried to sleep upright through the wail.

* * *

In the frozen night Slone woke to the hue of flame in the window, alight at the other end of the mining camp, something burning along the bluff. He dressed in the dark and descended the stairs by feel—the chatty woman nowhere seen or heard—and outside through the deepfreeze he made his way along the center road, huts and cabins now in arrant darkness. Some homes were no more than caves hewed into the base of the bluff, one with an oven door for a window, others with oval entrances wrapped in moose hide.

Slone saw the hunter, fifty or fifty-five years old, hardened by decades of walking and mining—he could see it in his stance. The hunter stood in the wide glow of the blaze: pallets, crates, boxes, pieces of tree. Donned wholly in gray wolf pelt, with white man's skin and untrimmed hair still dark despite his age, he seemed a make-believe shaman. The wolf's tail was still attached to his guise, its fanged head pulled low over his own for a hood.

When he saw Slone approach he turned to grin and welcome him to the heat. His teeth looked like stream-bottom pebbles beneath the still gallant fangs of the wolf he'd killed.

"I thought this would get your attention. Maud said we had a young traveler tonight. I knew it was you."

"You're not an Indian."

"Not officially."

"You're not a priest."

"In my own way I am, same as you and everyone."

"I'm no priest."

"Have it your way, then."

Long laminated scars embossed his forehead and face—the admonition of a grizzly. The beast had taken a piece of his nose and upper lip as token.

"Why did she come to you?"

"Step closer here. It won't hurt you, this fire. I like a big fire all after freeze-up. As reminder, you know. Breakup is still a long way off."

Fixed to a vertical spit in the blaze was a haunch of lynx or wolf he rotated with a ski pole. Above, the firmament was masked by its floor of cloud. A new storm was coming by daylight. This fire augmented with dark the surrounding night. The lard of the haunch cracked in the flame and Slone's airy gut yawned. The wind raised the bonfire and sent sparks in flight like insects aglow.

"I knew you'd be starved, traveling up from Keelut. Maud said you didn't eat. We're out of bread here, you know. Hank ain't been in with the plane. But we got meat to go 'round. For now." He paused to turn the spit. "Prey is real scarce this winter. Nothing I've seen before. You hungry?"

Slone looked at the meat in the blaze but said nothing.

"I got some potatoes too. I cooked them for us. You're welcome to one."

The roasting fatty scent of meat nearly stumbled Slone with

hunger. With a hay pick the hunter unloaded the haunch onto a grease-stained square of plywood.

"Come eat," he said.

His cave had been burrowed into the rock bluff by machine. It stayed lit with kerosene lamps that cast demonic shapes about the concave space, the air dense with the smell of wood smoke. His crude kiln was a steel drum torched open on one side, twelve feet of stovepipe snaking over to the entrance—Slone had to duck to enter—and fastened with wire and galvanized concrete nails hammered into the rock. It threw a dry sauna heat that engulfed the cave.

The hunter dwelled among the heaped and hanging bones of every beast born here, brown and black hides stacked like carpets at a market. A row of *National Geographic* and *Playboy* magazines, decades old, sat piled by a mattress gnawed on by rodents. A Ken doll in a string noose, hanging from a hook. On a wall the chasmal jaws of a bear trap. Wolf skulls by the score. Dozens of wolfish masks made of driftwood and dyed in ochre—they scowled from the wall and rounded vault. The masks were identical to what he'd found beneath Medora's pillow.

The hunter stripped from his costume to socks and briefs, his bare body muscled and scarred. He had the torso and limbs of a swimmer, though his face proclaimed every day of five decades. Slone sweated fast in the rolling heat of the fire and removed his parka. He sat opposite the hunter, cross-legged on a grizzly skin, eating burned potato and lynx meat from an earthen plate.

There beside the bed of pelts were Medora's boots, leather and fur, size eight, ordered from a catalog before freeze-up last season. The hunter saw Slone looking at the boots.

"I fixed her a new pair, mukluks with moose and wolf, waterproof lining, knee-high, real good ones. Those ones there are no good where she's going."

Slone chewed and nodded. The hunter's two bolt-action rifles and a single-barrel shotgun poked out from a crate, hunting knives piled on a tree-stump table.

"She knows you're coming for her. She told me that. She told me too what she did. That's why she came to me, to answer your question. Counsel, you can call it. She had one of my masks. I don't know how. I give them away to whoever comes through here and they seem to find who needs them. One way or another. You're welcome to one. It releases the wolf in you, boy. The wolf we all have in us."

They ate more in silence.

"How are you from this region, I wonder, with all that yellow hair? You look like a Nordic to me. The woman too. She has your same hair, but a whiter yellow, and she has your face too, I'd say. Ever notice how people who live together for a long while start to resemble each other? That's why I live alone. I don't want to look like nobody but me."

"You let her go from here."

"It's not my business what she did. There's no decree in the country. It don't reach here. I help who comes asking me. What brings them here and where they go to is nothing to me. I've seen plenty of mothers kill their young. You see it out here a lot."

He passed Slone a wooden jug of water with no handle, chill despite the warmth in the room. Slone drank it half gone and passed it back.

"I remember you, traveler. I remember your father too, when he came here with you. You were a little tyke then, maybe five or six. Don't you remember that?"

"Why did we come here?"

"To see me. Your father wanted a wolf's oil. He wouldn't shoot one himself. So he came to me for the oil. It was for you, this oil. Did you know that? Your father said you were unnatural. Said you had unnatural ways about you. That was his word, *unnatural*. An Indian witch from your village told him a wolf's oil could cure you, make you normal. Did it work? Are you normal now? I gave him the oil."

He sliced off another portion of lynx and laid it on Slone's plate.

"What'd your father mean, you were unnatural? What's unnatural about you, boy? You look wholesome enough to me."

"My father is dead. I am alive."

"Me too. My ancestors on the Yukon worshipped the wolf as a god, you know."

"Your ancestors are white like mine."

"On the outside, that's true."

"It's an odd people who will butcher their god."

"Kill your god and you become your god. For survival, not sport, of course. Look at where you are."

"I see sport here."

"I trade them pelts with Hank. He can sell them at the city, mostly marten and lynx he wants. They fetch a good price for him, more than wolverine or wolf. He trades me provisions, brings whatever I might need for the season. That's called a living, not a sport, I'd say."

"Tell me where she is."

"It's not for me to tell. I'll feed and clothe a traveler but I don't meddle. Meddle is for others. There's no meddle here. The animals and weather have their rules and I obey those."

They finished their meal without words. The hunter pressed tobacco into a pipe and passed it to Slone. From a flagon he poured moonshine the color and scent of gasoline. When Slone drank from it the liquid hollowed his sternum, sprawled in flame across his stomach. They smoked in quiet. Slone looked to the large hide hanging behind him, a shape and texture and tint he'd never seen before, neither bear nor moose nor caribou. He asked about its origin.

The hunter grinned, flecks of meat packed between his teeth. "Do you like a story, traveler?"

"I like the truth."

"The truth. Every story is the truth," and he laughed the smoke loose from his nose. "Okay. I'll tell you. It was '85 when I shot it. Early winter just before freeze-up. About a mile west of here, coming down a ridge into a ravine. Everything dusted with snow but not that hard cold of January yet. The ravine still running. It looked like a brown bear from the crest of the ridge. They'll stand on their hind legs, you know, to reach up a tree. And I saw it that way, standing. But then the path dipped down and around and when I had a clear view again, maybe eight minutes later, it was still standing. No brown bear stands that long. And through the glasses I saw it, its face gorilla, but not. A sagittal crest like one of them Neanderthals in the *National Geographic* pictures. Overall, I'd say, it was six hundred pounds easy but with the body shape of a human. You can see from that skin there behind you it was over seven feet in height."

Slone turned to look, then handed the pipe back to the hunter.

"But it was the eyes that got me. They were human eyes. Larger, of course, but human in every way. Its gaze, I mean. It was aware, *self*-aware. It was the Kushtaka. I heard about it all through my youth and there it was, clear as the day around me. It had a young one with it. With her, it was a female, I could see the teats. Young one about five feet, less hairy. Its face like any child's you'd see. A little monkey nose. But already muscular. Round with muscles, and it just a little thing. They were at the water drinking and it seemed she was teaching the young one something. About fish, I thought. And then pointing up into the tree at birds but I couldn't see what kind. The son of a bitch had speech. The damnedest thing."

He raised the pipe, took the smoke down deep into himself.

"This was a once-in-a-lifetime, as you can guess. I was a good eighty feet away but on my belly in thin snow and camouflaged real good in wolf down. Any wind there was in that ravine was against me, so they couldn't smell a thing. I had a .308 Winchester then, you know, the finest rifle ever made. It took that young one's head half off. The mother saw it before she heard it. Then she howled. Some sound, I have to tell you. Not like a wolf but a man's howl. It was the damnedest thing: half in the water, she tried to hold the young one's head together, where it was split, as if she could undo what been done. Of course she couldn't. And she just howled, look-ing up and around like it was lightning that did it. I dropped her right there, with the young one in her arms, right through the heart. You can't get a better shot than that."

He paused to finger more tobacco from a pouch.

"I had a sled with me on the ridge top but I couldn't fit them both on it. I mean, I couldn't tote all that weight, heavy bastards. I tried going back that night for the young one but the wolves had their dinner of it. And I ate all winter of the mother. A pork taste, I'd say, not like moose or bear. Not gamy like wolf. The strength that meat gave me, the spirit of the Kushtaka in me . . . I can't explain it. I had orgasms just standing here, not stroking myself, nothing like that at all. Just standing. I saved the eyes too, those amazing eyes. They're around here somewhere."

Slone drank again from the mug and they finished the last of the tobacco. Soon he rose and went slowly over to Medora's boots. He squatted and brought one to his face and inhaled the sweat-strong fur.

"You're welcome to the woman's boots. They're yours, really. I don't meddle."

Slone returned the boot and stood. On a low table there among bullets and tools was the key to Medora's truck fastened to a key ring Bailey had made at school: a smiley-faced heart of fired clay painted over in scarlet gloss. Slone held up the key, dangled it in the jumping firelight for the hunter to see.

"Yes. I traded her trucks. She took my Ford. I got the better of the deal, I'd say, for that Chevy. But the Ford is a damn good truck too. She didn't want her vehicle spotted on roads, I'm guessing. I don't like to meddle. Told her just take mine, I'd trade her, an even swap. Plus the boots I made her."

Slone removed the key ring, felt its polished flat weight in his palm, ran a thumb over its surface, then slid it down into a pocket. He said nothing.

Inching along the ribbed wall of the cave, he examined the wolf masks in museum display, each one crafted to look hellish and rabid.

"You're welcome to any of them masks there. Have your pick of them. It's not my business but I can see you need to let your wolf out a little. When's the last time you showed the monster in you, boy?"

Slone chose the black mask with elongated snout and overlarge fangs. With the leather straps he fastened it to his face through his yellow wreath of hair.

The hunter was bent now over the stove, adding a wedge of wood, and when he turned he seemed ready to say something. But

Slone was in the mask with a knife gripped by the blade, handle aimed at the hunter.

They stood that way regarding one another, their fire-thrown shadows towering about the cave. Seconds later the blade pierced the hunter's chest to the handle, just above the aorta. Midway between them in the air the blade had caught the quick glint of fire-light. In a gasp the hunter looked at the handle stuck to his chest, then at the upright animal across the cave. It seemed he wanted to ask yet another question he'd just lost the language for.

He needed both hands to yank out the blade. The coin-slot wound was black and withholding blood. He stood inspecting the knife almost in admiration of its design and the blood began seeping from the slot. Still gasping, he glanced at the monster in the mask. He stepped to the grizzly skin and collapsed on his back, waiting for what more would come.

Then Slone was above him, handgun aimed at the hunter's hairline, his own breath wet within the wolf face. Through the eye-holes of the mask he could see the hunter blinking and breathing, asthmatic, his lips trying to speak to whatever god he claimed for his own. Slone put the bullet in the hunter's forehead and watched the hole ooze a blackish blood.

He walked back into the polar night with Medora's boots beneath his arm, the mask still fastened to his face.

VII

Cheeon started shooting as soon as Marium reached the line of vehicles in front of his cabin. He didn't know the make of rifle Cheeon had in the attic but it was without stop, ripping cup-sized holes through the trucks. He could not fathom why a man would have a weapon like that, how he'd even go about getting one. He looked over to a cop to tell him to duck, duck lower, then saw a piece of his face and skull tear off in sherbet under his helmet. He ducked then and fell dead.

The rounds came faster than he'd ever seen or heard. He could see the flame from the long barrel in the attic window. It pivoted smoothly up and down, right and left, attached to a tripod. Cheeon wasn't quitting to reload. He didn't need to. The windshields and windows of the trucks were shattering, spraying over Marium, the men, the ground. Air hissing from shot tires. Rounds clunking into engine blocks, dull but loud like hammer hits.

When Cheeon turned the gun to the nearby pines the rounds trimmed off branches, hacked the bark through. The snow showered down in great mist. The men in those trees fell dead to the

ground with branches and snow. He couldn't hear any men return-
ing even a single round. They were crouched close to the earth,
hands over their heads despite their helmets. Those who weren't
shot dead looked amazed that this was happening to them. Or that
such a thing was even possible at this place.

He crawled over to the end of the nearest truck, beneath the
back bumper. He waited there with the carbine for a break in the fire,
for Cheeon to reload. But it'd been a minute or more and the lead
would not stop. He thought that soon one of the trucks would catch
fire and blow, that they'd all be burnt or worse. He could aim at the
attic window from beneath the bumper. He fired there, splintering
the wood of the cabin. Maybe getting a round or two inside at him.
He just couldn't tell.

Cheeon's fire broke for several seconds, then started again at
the truck Marium was under. The lead piercing the truck sounded
again like quick hits with a hammer. He didn't know what they
were doing to the fuel tanks. He could see the rounds erupting in
snow beneath the truck, hear them against the chassis. And once
more he just could not understand why this man would have that
weapon here. What purpose it was supposed to serve other than
this one upon them.

He crawled back around, crouched behind a wheel, saw a man
try to dash to a spruce where another flailed, yelling. This man was
hit halfway there, his blood flaring bright against the white before
he fell sideways. His insides spilled, steamed there pink in the snow.

A minute more of this and Cheeon quit. Whether to reload or
just watch all he'd done, Marium could not know. At the left flank
of the cabin a man shielded by spruce began firing at the alcove. It
must have been his service pistol—the pop-pop discharge sounded
pitiful after the barrage they'd just heard. Marium hollered for him

to hold his fire. He knew as soon as Cheeon saw where the rounds were coming from he'd mow down those trees and that man along with them.

The trucks were perforated, made of tinfoil. He yelled again for everyone to stay low. A man was facedown near him, by the exhaust pipe, in an oval of his own blood. Marium turned him over and saw that the rounds had gone through his flak jacket, into his throat. This man hadn't had even a second for a last tally. Marium heard himself yelling again—for someone to get on the radio, the satellite phone, something, to call in backup. But no one responded to him.

He could tell they didn't want to move at all. Someone he couldn't see, whose voice he didn't recognize, yelled for a doctor. It was an odd request, he thought, since there wasn't a doctor among them or coming. No doctor who could undo what was being done here. Then Cheeon's fire hit where this man lay and the voice abruptly quit calling.

He saw Arnie there on the ground with his carbine. He crawled near him and said his name. Arnie looked at him as if trying to remember who Marium was. Or what Marium might have to do with this alien thing now pressed upon him. He said Arnie's name again, could see the shock in his eyes. Shock always looks the same, he knew—a cross between surprised and sleepy.

Arnie wouldn't respond. Marium slapped him then, hard on the face, and was ashamed at the force of his hand. The snot flew slant from Arnie's nostrils and he seemed embarrassed by this. He wiped his nose with a glove and the snot froze there in a white streak. He began blinking, swallowing, and Marium knew then that he'd come around.

"Are you hearing me now, Arnie? Arnie, goddamn it, please look at me."

"I hear you."

"You see those rocks there?"

He pointed behind them at the uneven row of boulders beside a snowed-in patch of spruce. Arnie looked to the boulders and nodded.

"You're gonna go to them, get behind them. I'll cover you as you go. Are you hearing me?"

"I am. I'm hearing you, Don."

"Don't run till I start unloading, but when I do, run quick, please. As soon you get there stay low between that dip there, between those two big ones, you see there? You see where I mean, Arnie? Please look, goddamn it."

"I'm looking. I see it."

"Then I'll let up, and as soon as you hear me stop I want you to train that rifle on the window and don't let off the trigger till you see me reach the cabin, the right side of it. The right side. Am I clear?"

"It's clear, boss."

"Is that magazine full?"

"It's full."

"Please check. Check right now."

"It's full."

"You have others in that vest?"

Arnie felt his vest as you might feel for your wallet. "I have them," he said. "They're right here."

Marium saw that the lap of his pants was soaked through with urine. On the hood of the truck sat an unshot cup of coffee, smoking there with the lid off, waiting for someone to come sip from it.

"You ready, Arnie? Are you ready now?"

"Yes. Yes, I am."

"You haul ass to those boulders as soon as I start, and when you get there unload on the son of a bitch and please don't stop till you see me reach the cabin. Do not let off on that window but for Christ's sake watch me too, okay, to make sure I've reached the cabin before you stop. Tell me you understand."

"I understand. I'll do it, boss."

"You do it, Arnie. His weapon can't go through boulders, you understand that? Stay behind the rocks."

"I'll do it."

Marium motioned to the others, to those who were left, those looking at him. Motioned to hold their fire. He crawled beneath the back bumper of the second vehicle in their line. He began unloading on the upstairs window full auto. He hoped the rounds would last in time for Arnie to make the row of rocks. Arnie couldn't spare those few seconds it'd take Marium to load in another magazine. The rounds dislodged snow from the cabin roof, which slid down and off in a powdered sheet.

In a minute he was empty. Cheeon knew it and trained fire on him then. The rounds filled the wheel well, loud near Marium's face. They hit the rear axle as he crawled backward from beneath the truck. When he was clear he looked himself over for blood.

From the boulders Arnie began shooting hard at the cabin. Cheeon waited it out. When he did, Marium sprinted, out of view of the attic window. Slipping, falling in ice and snow. Crashing heavy onto both elbows, his stomach onto the stock of the carbine, the wind kicked from him. He struggled to breathe. Between a gap in their trucks he saw Arnie's fire stop. Marium showed him a thumbs-up but didn't know if Arnie saw or not. And then Cheeon started in on him, the rounds sparking against the boulders, chipping off shards in a thin cloud of snow and rock dust.

From this side of Cheeon's cabin he could see up the central road of the village. Sled dogs everywhere howled madly in their kennels. People stood in front of their doors and vehicles. He motioned for them to get back inside. They didn't move at all. He thought for some reason that one of them might start shooting at him with a hunting rifle.

Cheeon's rear door was locked. Marium waited for Cheeon's gun to start again before elbowing through a pane of glass. One step in and his boot screeched wet on the pine flooring. He stopped, looked down to lever off the boots onto the mat. And he saw there in the weak gray light what looked like a fishing line strung taut across the room, a foot off the floor. It passed through an eye screw in the baseboard, up the wall and through another eye screw in the crown molding. Over to a pistol-grip twelve-gauge fixed into the corner above the door, behind him, angled down at his head. The trip line girded to its trigger.

The sight of that shotgun, knowing how close he'd just come, felt less like relief than loss. He snipped the line with scissors in a Swiss army knife and felt sure then that he'd be carried from this cabin in a bag.

He squatted there and tried to breathe but his breath would not come. He could hear and feel the gun above in the attic. It vibrated through the walls and floor beams—a buzz that came into his bones. He didn't know if more men were being hit outside. He thought of the phone call to Susan that Cheeon assured him of when they'd spoken at his door. For many seconds he considered fleeing. Considered waiting for backup. Or else trying to burn this goddamn place to cinders.

There wasn't anything else to be thought. He'd talked to guys about moments like these. Guys with him on the special unit down in Juneau. Guys from the service who knew. And everyone said the same thing to him: for all we pride ourselves on thinking, at a crossroads with the devil, thinking falls to feeling and feeling starts you moving.

As he squatted there he tried to stay the shakes in his limbs. Then crept in, quiet in his socks, to see where the stairs were. His coat made a nylon scratch beneath the arms when he moved. He peeled it off, let it drop. And there on a hook was a little girl's pink-hooded jacket, some girlish cartoon thing grinning at him.

Out the front window he could see snow exploding where the rounds smashed the ground, could hear the thunking of lead on metal. Ten steps led up to the attic. Each one took him more time than he needed or wanted. He felt odd in his socks, as if a man had to be wearing boots in order to do this. He knew he couldn't make the stairs creak. Cheeon had quit shooting—there wasn't a sound anywhere in the cabin or out.

Three steps from the top he could see Cheeon through the spindles of the railing. He was there smoking at the window of this sharply angled space. The ceiling low enough to touch. The weapon fastened to a tripod bolted into the floor—an M60 machine gun, Marium thought, used in helicopters, on Humvees. Next to it a five-foot heap of ammunition, enough to shoot nonstop all day, into the night if he wanted. Hanging all through the room was the strong scent of the gun. A smell close to the clean oil on new engines, almost pleasant. Hundreds of spent shells scattered the floor, and many rolled to the stairs. Again he could not comprehend where this gun had come from or why.

Marium was level with Cheeon now, over the top step, the carbine trained on his back. He said Cheeon's name. Cheeon did not tense with surprise, did not turn around right away. He stood there smoking, nodding, surveying all he'd done. He took his time with it.

"They didn't do so well down there, guy."

"Turn, Cheeon. Let me see your hands. Let me see 'em now."

"My hands? Your voice sounds strange, guy. You okay?"

"Turn, Cheeon. Arms out."

Marium thought: *I will shoot you through the back, you son of a bitch.* Honor, some code of conflict—they did not apply here now.

Cheeon turned then, still smoking, his hands not out. One held the cigarette, the other in a back jeans pocket. Marium had expected a crazed, sweaty face. But Cheeon looked just as he had earlier when they'd talked at his door. He looked like a man resigned to things. A man who had just ended ten or more lives and was okay with wherever that truth placed him on the spectrum before his unsaving god.

Marium knew Cheeon wasn't walking out of this cabin. His legs quit quaking then because he understood that he himself wasn't going to die here.

"You stopped that phone call for today," Cheeon said. "That phone call to your wife. But it's coming, ain't it? That phone call's always coming."

"Your hands, Cheeon. Put them out. Now."

When Cheeon took his right hand slowly from his back pocket, Marium saw the nickel of the handgun. Cheeon didn't raise it at him. Just let Marium see it. Let it hang there at his side against his jeans, tapping it as if to a tune of his own making. The other hand still busy with that cigarette in his lips. His eyes squinting at Marium through smoke.

Marium shot at him full auto. It thrust him back into the open window. The handgun and cigarette dropped to Cheeon's feet. Marium shot at him more until he fell through and landed on the snow in front of his door. He went to the window and looked down at Cheeon on his back. His eyes were open still and it seemed he was looking. Looking at a wan sky that would not receive him.

* * *

More men arrived—men he knew, some he did not. They searched the village for Slone, for hint of him, but the villagers told them nothing. They found an old woman in her hut, dead in a rocker, a knife wound clean through her throat. No one in Keelut would tell them anything about this old woman. They found no papers, no verification of her name or age, of who she was or had been.

They moved on through the village and found nothing. When they returned to the old woman's hut to retrieve her she'd been stolen, spirited away for concealment. Or for what else Marium could not know. They checked the village again but could not find her or those who had taken her. He remembered Cheeon telling him, just one hour earlier, that they weren't alike—not the two men, not this village and the town. Marium knew then that Cheeon was right and wondered what else he was right about.

Hours later, after dark, at the small hospital in town—confusion because nobody there had seen anything close to this before. Wounds they could not make sense of. To Marium it seemed a good thing there was nothing to be done because the staff wouldn't have been able to do it. Those who died, died in a mess. Those who didn't walked away unscratched on the outside. The dead had been frozen, stuck to the ground by their blood and entrails. They had to be scraped off the earth with shovels, or else pried up with pickaxes. Marium and the men loaded the bodies in bags into two pickup trucks. Half had been brought here to the hospital and the other half to the morgue, a mix-up he tried to explain.

Not all were back yet from Keelut. Family members of police paced the hospital hallways, unsure who was living and who not. Some spouses wailed, wolflike, when news reached them. Siblings saw Marium come through the emergency entrance in squeaking boots. They clung to him with questions.

"Christ, Don," someone said, "they told us you were killed."

He couldn't guess what *they* he meant but showed this man he was alive by standing there and simply pointing to himself.

Arnie's wife was there too. Marium reassured her and she thanked him, grabbed his hand hard, as if he had been the one who'd kept her husband living. Marium had to tell some of these family members to go to the morgue because that was where their husbands and brothers now were. Others he told to go to the station to wait because their guys would be there, alive, before long.

In the men's room of the hospital he knelt and wept, holding the sink for balance. Bent over a water fountain, he drank hungrily for more than a minute, the water too cold over his throat. He could see the snow melting pink beneath his boots, ice pellets of blood crammed in the soles.

Through a clutch of nurses, of doctors, he saw her auburn hair on a bench. When the clutch dispersed he saw her sitting, not blinking at the wall opposite, her face licked by grief, faint mascara trails over her cheekbones. It was only the two of them at that end of the hallway now. She seemed to sense him standing there because she turned. And what came from her then was a quick snort and a smile, almost a laugh, a quick shake of her head before she turned away again and sobbed.

He sat beside her and held her. She didn't say anything. He buried his face into her hair while she pounded his chest and shoulders. And she kept pounding as they sat there.

"I tried calling. I couldn't get you."

"Goddamn it, we need you, goddamn it."

He knew then the *we* she meant, and he held her again and said, "I'm here."

* * *

Later that night as she lay sleeping, he sat in his chair and smoked by the cracked window, watched her in the quarter light. He could not know if she was dreaming or how she felt to have such life inside her. But it seemed also the only possible cure for what had happened this day. He'd heard others talk of the numbness after such things, but he felt no numbness now. What he felt was tired through to the marrow, thick through the head as if a cold were coming on. But not numb. Numb would have let him sleep, but sleep just then seemed a peace he'd not soon have again. It was a rare kind of torture, he knew, to be so tired and unable to sleep. He smoked for an hour, waiting for yawns that never came.

That old woman in the village, upright in her rocking chair: Slone had cut her throat straight through to the spine. And that was Marium's dread as he looked at his sleeping wife and the child inside her. The dread that there are forces in this world you cannot digest or ever hope to have hints of.

There was somebody's whispered voice in his head, in the quiet of their bedroom, keeping him awake. He thought it was Cheeon's voice. He had not wanted to do what Cheeon made him do. Killing a man can mean more for the killer than it does for the man killed.

Cheeon had let his pistol dangle there in his hand, in the attic of the cabin he'd built with that hand. He let Marium see it, didn't even have to raise it at him—he just knew. He'd prepared, waited for this, with that machine gun, the tripod bolted to the floor. And it all played out as he had wished. Marium gave him what he'd wanted. And for that he felt shame.

VIII

A strong late summer rain seemed to signal the end of morning. Slone and Bailey were barefoot, shirtless in the cooling shower, single file on narrow hill paths, side by side on wider ones. They wound up and down the trail to stand on shaded boulders at the banks of the storm-gorged creek. The risen current rushed, its surface in full boil. Mosquitoes chased away by storm. They sat on the rock overhang, dangled their legs knee-deep in the creek. In minutes the downpour softened through the sheaved tops of trees and the dripping world grew silent again.

"Mama said you're going away," the boy said.

"In a few months. Not so soon."

"Mama said a long time."

"A year, maybe a little less. Deployment is that long. You remember deployment?"

"No."

"It means work. It means money for us."

"We need money?"

"Yes."

"Mama said money doesn't matter."

"We don't need much. But we need it."

"She said you can get money here."

"Not lately I can't. No one can. It's my duty to go there."

"What's duty?"

"It means when you're good at something, and something needs to be done, you have to go do it."

"For my birthday I'll be seven."

"I know. It seems a long time. It's not so long. I'll be back when you're seven and a half."

Normally clear to its sand bottom, this water had turned dark, dense in its quick swell downstream. A tree limb bobbed closely by like an arm reaching out for rescue. Bailey reached forth his own arm to touch it and Slone held the boy's belt loop.

"I can swim."

"I know you can swim. It's moving fast today."

"Mama said men kill people in war."

"You have to, yes."

"You killed a person before. When I was in mama's belly."

"Who told you that?"

"Somebody."

"Okay, somebody. Somebody who?"

"Somebody."

Clamor of thunder and then the shuffling of it behind them, so muted it might be above the Yukon or else far into the core of Canada.

"It's bad to kill people but not bad to kill the caribou."

"Yes. The caribou keep us alive. Sometimes it's necessary to kill a person too, if you have to keep alive."

"What's necessary?"

"If you have no other choice."

"You had no other choice."

"No."

"You did it to keep us alive?"

"To keep us safe, yes."

"Who did you kill?"

"A man who would hurt Mama and you."

"But he didn't hurt us?"

"No. I hurt him first."

"And no one missed him?"

"I don't know that. It wasn't my job to ask that. Only to protect you and Mama."

"No one told on you?"

"No one told on me. No one would dare. The village is our family. Do you understand what that means?"

"Yes."

"Do you?"

"Yes."

"It means you can count on them. If something's wrong, or if you have a secret to keep, you count on them to help. That's what it means."

"Who?"

"Who what?"

"Who did you hurt?"

"A man who came into our village. He was a drifter."

"What's drifter?"

"Like driftwood. See there? That driftwood? It means a wanderer without a home."

The current's cool swiftness on their calves came close to massage. The whey sky seemed to sharpen all the green around them.

"How?"

"How did I hurt him, you mean?"

"Yes."

"With a knife."

"You like your knife," and he turned to smile up at his father. He then smacked the water with a stick and Slone held tight to the boy's belt loop.

"Mama said Cheeon helped you."

"Cheeon helped me."

"He's my family?"

"Yes."

"He's my friend?"

"Always. You're full of questions today."

Across the creek a buck and its doe moved through alders dripping in the storm's stay. Slone pointed for the boy to look and, not speaking, they looked until the deer ducked from view.

"It felt good to kill my first deer," the boy said.

"You're a good shot with the Remington."

"It felt good and bad at the same time."

"Don't feel bad. You fed two whole families that night."

"My teacher said people aren't deer because people are equal. She said to kill any people is bad."

"You'll hear that a lot."

"My teacher said that."

"I know. It's what they say. It's a lie."

"It's not a lie."

"There are good people who won't hurt you and there are bad people who will. Ask your teacher if those are equal, if good equals bad."

"It's good to kill bad people?"

"If you have to."

"Like that man who wanted to hurt Mama?"

"Like him, yes. The creek is cold today."

"My feet are cold."

This spot on the rock at the water was where the boy would come to think of his father.

"I'll be with you while I'm gone. Do you know what that means?"

"Yes."

"Do you really?"

"No."

"It means that even when we're not together I'll still be with you. I'll be right here with you."

He placed two fingers on the boy's pale bird chest, his skin a see-through sheath.

"When you're away you'll still be with me?"

"Yes."

"No you won't," the boy said. "Don't lie."

And soon the hard shower began again.

* * *

The wastrel, another vagabond, appeared in Keelut one winter afternoon from where no one could know. Refugee from the pipeline, from a boarded-up mine or bust highway plan. Scrounger who still dreamt of gold in some missed gulch of this land. Backpack and blanket an earthen hue from the earth itself. Wind-lashed skin and a mane part mullet, hands coarse from the weather this wild place gave. Footwear fashioned from a hide no one recognized and tied down with twine.

The loamed-over face was creased from winter toil but his eyes beneath thatched brows kept the burn of youth, an unnamed liquid shade on pause from blue to green. Impossible to guess age in such a patchwork face. He carried with him a lever-action relic with a duct-taped leather strap and scope. Some of his clawed-at clothes looked sewn shut with dental floss.

At the hem of the village before the first snowfall he stood at the line of spruce and could barely be seen but for his breath. At night his campfire shone through the boles and at the first glow of day he could be seen loitering in the village as if waiting to be asked an inquiry or else handed meat.

On the second afternoon the vagrant sat against a boulder twenty yards in front of the Slones' cabin and watched the door. Slone and Medora studied him from a window, Medora eight months round and long past ready to have their child out. Each morning she woke with knowledge of her body's new districts. Knowledge of what she soon must do and the doubt of whether or not she could do it. The terror of what it would do to her.

"Another drifter," she said. "On his way west, probably."

"He ain't west enough yet."

"He looks hungry too."

"That look on him is more than hunger."

"Bring him something, Vernon. It won't hurt to give him bread and maybe some cheese."

"He's got that rifle. He looks able to hunt for himself."

They stood looking for many minutes, the child heeling against the walls of her womb.

"Bring him something so he'll go."

Slone approached the vagrant with slices of cheese and bread in a bag. This close he could see the discolored sections of skin on his fingers and nose, the scars of frequent frostbite—they looked part bruise, part burn. Hands slightly swollen from constant freeze and thaw. The smell on him was pungent campfire, something charred. His pants were sealskin, made on the coast in another time, worn through in places as testament to a thousand miles of amble. The loose ruff of wolf hair at the top of a ragged parka drooped from his throat to show a necklace, a white stone rune of a horse.

"This home interest you, guy?" Slone crouched to him eye-level and passed the bag of food. The man placed it onto his lap without looking inside.

"A new boy arrives next month," he said.

His teeth looked like cubes of shattered plate glass, ill-fit as if each tooth had come from a different skull.

"Someone tell you it's a boy? No one told us."

"Feels like a boy to me."

"You and whatever you feel need to move on from here. There's bread and cheese for you. It's dropping low tonight and the first snows are coming."

"Termination dust won't come on tonight. We got a night or two more before that."

"You're a weatherman too?"

"You could say I know a little something about weather and what's coming. Do you have a name?"

"My name's got no meaning to you."

"Not yours. Do you have a name for the boy?"

"That's got no meaning to you either." He leaned in toward the man. "You eat that bread and cheese and then you and that rifle are gone from here. I don't care where you go, but you go there. If you're needing a ride to town or beyond to the city you wait on the road. Someone will be going that way before long. Stick out your thumb and someone will stop for you."

"It looks warm inside," he said, not looking at Slone.

"You should think about a home for yourself, then."

"I mean your woman. Looks warm inside her. Makes me miss the womb."

Slone turned to see Medora half veiled by a curtain at the window, her belly protruding, and he turned back to the vagrant.

"I want you to look into my face now. Look good. I want you to believe me when I say this: I will end your every day. Do you believe me? Do you believe me when I say that to you?"

Above them a passel of ravens erupted from the keep of trees like black memories freed, their wings in wild applause.

"I believe that boy has got a short life."

"Mention my child again and you'll see how short your own is."

The vagabond took a toothpick from a pocket and began working it between his cuspids.

"My granddad was on the Skagway trail," he said. "Up in the White Pass, back in 1897. He was fourteen, trying to get to the Klondike. Trying to pass over to the Yukon before freeze-up."

"They were after gold," Slone said.

"You bet they were. Sweet gold. They all were greedy with it. Thousands of men were on the trail at once, just a narrow footpath, with thousands of horses and mules too. More than fifty miles of narrow switchbacks, over rivers and them mean summits, through some godforsaken mires. And that trail was just clogged right up. No one could move, all those horses and people. They sat there for days at a time, not moving, some freezing to death, some starving. Disease too."

He pressed one nostril shut and fired a nub of snot from the other. It landed on his knee and he picked it off and scraped it into his mouth.

"Place there called Devil's Hill," he said. "The trail on the cliffs was just a few feet wide. Wide enough for a man only. Them bastards tried to bring the horses and they just dropped straight down, fell real fast from all the pack weight. Hundreds of feet down, crashed dead onto the rocks. Fifteen, twenty at a time. What do you think about that?"

Slone said nothing.

"You know how many of them thousands of horses survived the Skagway trail that year?" the wastrel said. "Zero. Granddad told me about piles of dead horses, huge stinking heaps of them, all their eyes pecked out by ravens. Fell into crevasses, worked right to death. Broke legs or drowned in them rivers. And they rotted there among them people. Just rotted right in front of them. A god-awful stink."

With a black fingernail he picked at his nostril for another nub of snot.

"You know what Granddad said to me? Said most of them horses were committing suicide. Imagine that. Them horses were throwing themselves off cliffs two hundred feet high, hurling themselves over to end their torture from that trail. He could see it in their eyes, their will for death, for self-destruction. Now, can you believe something such as that?"

Slone studied his face a final time and stood. "You've got till night to be gone from here. Remember my words."

"You remember too," the wastrel said.

In from the clamp of cold, Slone bolted the door. He went to Medora at the window.

"He'll leave soon," he said.

"He was staring at me. What does he want?"

"Just food. He'll eat and leave."

"He's not eating," she said. "He's staring."

* * *

At dusk they saw the shine of the vagrant's campfire through trees. Medora stayed at the window as if held by hypnosis, summoned by the spell of a mage, her child low in her and still heeling for exit.

Hours later in bed Slone waited for her to pass over into sleep. He left soundlessly through the rear door and moved through the timber toward the vagrant's camp. In the clearing a World War II Army tent canted sharply at the sides. The hide of a hare splayed across sticks to dry before the crackling blaze. From the black of the woods he watched for movement, steadied his breath, watched more. He crept toward the tent and for minutes listened low to the ground. He could see or hear nothing of this man.

Avoiding shadows, he peeled the back side of the tent just enough, the hunting knife cocked to spear. But the tent was empty, the rank sleeping bag thrown open. He entered on his knees. The vagrant's rifle lay atop a blanket. Painted crudely on the inner fabric of the tent like Paleolithic cave art were horses disemboweled and eyeless. He felt the pictures with a finger and when he squinted closer saw that they had been limned in some prey's blood.

He dumped the vagrant's shoulder bag. Fouled socks and sweater. Jackknife, sardines, coffee. Ammunition, wooden matches, candles. Gun oil, compass, fishhooks. The mummified head of a marmot. A Mickey Mouse key chain without a single key. No paper or card telling of this man, of how he knew about Medora and their coming child. There beside the sleeping bag he found a figurine whittled expertly from driftwood—a woman gravid with child, breast-heavy and fanged. It was the fertility symbol of some predatory she-beast. It was, he somehow knew, meant to be Medora. And the nausea of dread lifted from his guts to his throat.

He sprinted then back to their cabin, bounding over fallen trees through a moonless night.

* * *

She lay half asleep, a dream mostly recollection:

The women of the village called her fortunate to be eight months at the start of winter instead of in the ninety-six degrees of last summer's heat, an August stifle they'd never known before in Keelut—a heat whose source seemed intent to maim them. Mosquitoes came in clouds and the villagers greased themselves in oils from wolf organs or beaver fat to keep the hordes of them at bay. They stood in the shade of poplars and simply looked at one another astonished, sweating as if some blight had been unleashed upon them. They went into the hills and down into the flume beneath canopies of cottonwood and sat in the cooling streambed for refuge from the heat and bugs. They didn't have memory, language, or myth for this heat, had never heard hint of it. The elderly whispered of curse, of punishment sent for the sins of the village.

Her eyes opened now and saw Slone's silhouette there in the bedroom doorway. She smelled campfire on him and something else, something raw, she could not say. She wondered why he had gone out in the cold at this witching hour of night. She said his name but he did not respond. The fear started then in her upper chest. She leaned for the lamp and as sudden as gunshot its light found the vagrant there, steady there in the room.

What unlatched in her just then was not terror, but an awareness of a riddle, or of cause and effect—of how the dawn cannot possibly know the plot of day's coming dark. Instinctively she put a hand on her belly, as if drawing his attention to two lives would rally his will to preserve them both. She questioned the protocol here, who should speak first or else if words had become altogether useless.

"There's food," she said. "There's money. In a jar. By the stove. There's fifty dollars in the jar."

"This boy can't live. Someone sent me to warn you."

She heard her odd words—mere creaks in the floor beams— asking who he was, what he wanted.

"The hag sent me to warn you," he said, his voice womanlike, almost calming. "This boy can't live. Stop his life and go back to the place you came from."

The questions she had for him would not find sound. Who had sent him? How did he know of them and their coming child? She looked to the window, thought of how quickly she'd have to move, to tear aside the curtains. To raise the pane and climb out. It wasn't cold enough yet for plastic sheeting on the windows but soon it would be.

His complexion was reddish in the orange shine of lamplight. He looked part Inuit: the straight bridge of nose, eyes pinched at their ends, mane a silken black. And because he did not advance, because he held no weapon, she had the smallest understanding that he had not come to harm her.

"What do you know about us?"

"I know what I need to know to warn you," he said.

From inside his parka he retrieved a painted object carved of driftwood. He turned it toward the lamplight for her to see—a shaman's wolf mask painted with red ochre. He advanced by careful steps and reached the mask to her but she would not take it, would not remove her hands from her belly. He placed the mask on the bed beside her and returned to the doorway.

"That mask is yours," he said. "Someone made it for you."

She looked to the mask rimmed with real wolf hair. When she was a girl her father told her that to kill a wolf was to kill a messenger from the gods who protected them.

"Wear the mask," the wastrel said, "and then you'll know what you have to do. That's what I was sent to tell you."

She felt the wood of the mask, traced the teeth with a finger. When she looked again to the vagrant she saw the flash of blade rise from behind him. It spiked up beneath his chin at an angle deep into his head. His eyes strained but stayed fixed on her, stubbornly alive. Slone twisted the blade and a gout of blackish blood broke from the vagrant's throat and mouth. It dumped onto the rug in wet clumps. His whole weight went limp on the hilt of the knife, then Slone pulled it sideways and severed his throat through to the spine.

Slone dropped him then. Medora felt the vagrant's body thump against the floor. She looked at Slone rained-on with blood and heaving with breath from the run. She knew then that more trouble could not be stopped.

Slone and Cheeon mopped the mess. She watched from the bed. Before they drove the wastrel into the valley Slone gave her a handgun—it was the same gun he'd taught her to shoot with when they were ten years old, firing at pumpkins on a fallen tree. He instructed her to shoot the next person who came through their door. "If that person isn't me," he added. All the while she sat up in bed with the wolf mask in her hands, on her belly, feeling the points of its whittled teeth.

When the men left, she raised the mask to her face and tied it on.

* * *

The boy was born at noon in their cabin, Medora assisted by her mother and village midwives, one of them Yup'ik. Her given name, long and guttural, had been truncated to Lu. She ordered Slone and Cheeon and the other men outdoors, where they smoked and paced, wordless and put-upon, hours yet from celebration, heavy from the fatigue of cold and waiting.

Twenty-two below zero and Lu instructed Medora's mother to open the windows and doors for the release of black spirits snared within these walls, to provide free passage for their ancestors, for them to enter, to bless, to aid in the arrival. In a corner, the hag rocked in a chair eating crackers, white crumbs stuck to her shawl, in one hand an amulet she'd fashioned from bone.

In front of the fire, on a woven circular rug covered with bed-sheets, the six women knelt, crouched about Medora with white towels and basins of water, a sterilized straight razor and shears. They gripped her limbs. Lu knelt bare-handed at the center in the leakage, singing her language no one could sing but still seemed to comprehend. The hag said nothing through this long torment, only crunched her crackers, rubbed her amulet and rocked.

Medora's mother had made a bone-colored paste of aloe and oils from a wolf's organs. Lu daubed it now thickly on Medora's center as the others talked her through this with directions to breathe and blow, the pressure in her anus like a phantom defecation.

The hearth heat and stink of fluid hung strong even with the open windows and doors. The women sweated prodding out the boy. Medora wept and yelled and looked to her mother as the bottom pressure built and would not abate. She thrashed her hair in their laps, crying she could not do it—it had been hours and she could not.

Lu motioned for two women to stand and each took a leg

behind the knee and pressed it back toward Medora. The pressure in her rent, Lu's naked fingers pulling her wide and shouting the same word no one but the hag knew. When the child crowned, Medora's cries cut through the village and the men outside knew it was soon.

The boy's oblong head was exposed now, turtle-like, slimed in silent squall. The birth cord was noosed about the neck, his body lodged there, bloodied in partial freedom despite Medora's pushing. Still crooning, Lu motioned for the razor while Medora bucked with her head back in her mother's lap, her eyes crimped closed. Another woman readied the morphine needle and plunged it fast into her hip.

Lu lifted, pulled at the child's head. With the razor she opened Medora one inch more. A rush of bright blood and Medora dropped limp into blackness while Lu pried a finger beneath the looped cord and stretched it away enough to cut through.

The child was unstuck now and with a pinkie Lu hooked into his mouth, trying to clear his airway. She then rinsed him there in the basin—his first cry a pule—as the others stanched Medora's bleeding with car-wash sponges and tied off the cord. When the placenta slid loose, Lu instructed a woman to place it in the hearth to burn as an offering to ancestors. The others sewed Medora closed.

"This child is cursed already," her mother said, and she and Lu looked to the hag in the corner but she was gone.

Lu attempted to latch the boy to Medora but his cries came wild now for lack of milk. On the sofa Lu sat and put the child to her own full breast—wet nurse and mother of eight, she was never dry—and the boy fed weakly first and then in greed.

At the front door a constellation of men's faces, Slone's uncertain between joy and dread. Lu waved him in, only him, and he stood over his son and could not believe his ample hair—he'd always thought babies bald. He went to Medora, unconscious on the rug. The women mending her looked up and waved him away in a gesture indicating all was well or would soon be. Medora's mother would not look at him.

When they finished, Slone carefully lifted Medora and carried her to their bedroom, where two women wrapped her in towels and down covers, then stayed with her through the day and night. Her mother stood at the window as if waiting, wanting something, some force to fly in and halt her daughter's woe. In the main room on the sofa Slone held his slumbering boy, this wrinkled elf he'd made, intoxicated by the taintless scent of his head, his breathing in the swaddle no different from that of a newborn pup.

"It almost killed her," her mother said to Slone. "Almost killed the both of them."

"She's alive," he said. "We're all alive."

An immense fire raged in a stone pit at the center of the village, revelers dancing around its forked girth. Yup'ik supplicants chanted, drummed in celebration, pleaded to gods and ancestors for this boy's weal. They tossed bags of tobacco into the flame for sacrifice, drinking from carafes of gin and joyous in the freeze. Sled dogs yelped at the noise. The crouching clouds promised more snow but the villagers danced undeterred. Women brought frozen char and bricks of caribou sawed from a meat pole. They cooked over barrels and soon everyone ate with blessings and thanks.

Slone would hold his boy daily, at daybreak and after twelve-hour toil in the mine, while Medora slept recovering, indifferent to the child who spurned her breast. Lu remained there in their cabin during daylight; Medora's mother and a Yup'ik woman stayed till dawn. Slone whispered to his wife but she would not whisper back. Some sinister force had seized her, a sorrow fed by fear—it responded to no balm he knew. Her appetite was gone, her voice distorted, and at night came the inscrutable mumbling of the half possessed, even as the child wailed from his room till the wet nurse fed him.

On his monthly rounds a young white doctor arrived from town to see Medora and the boy, to inspect the suture, take notes on a clipboard. With his good haircut and teeth, his city-bought clothes and boots, he was clearly not of this village. He left blue pain pills, syringes, more vials of morphine. He told Slone to give her one week more to rebound—some women, he said, spiral inside themselves postpartum.

"It will pass," Medora heard him say to Slone. She did not have the voice to tell this doctor that some afflictions can't pass.

What infected her was beyond all ransom, some warp in the fabric of things. As she lay for weeks in bed, turned to the ashen winter light at the window, she could not know what had been loosed within her, how her covenant with the world had been cut. Her mother and Slone and others seemed just dark streaks streaming in and out of rooms.

What she saw, she saw with fogged eyes—eyes somehow clouded over in distortion of all she knew. She saw peculiar eddies of dark and day. Sitting on the toilet was an agonizing effort, brushing her teeth and changing clothes impossible, the baby's pules very far from her, this new prison without clues of any kind.

Morphine plugged the rip in her, blocked all visions of the vagrant who had come to her in warning. Slone refused to give the morphine at night but Lu gave it twice daily while the baby slept. It was the only time Medora could stop staring at such pain. Her entire past seemed to point at this fray.

The vagrant failed to go away. She constructed false memories of him in her girlhood, could see him there in pockets of her past. Every wanderer who'd ever come through Keelut now had his gaze, his gait, his reek of wood smoke. Every one of them was now a harbinger of this day. In her opiate dreams she could see herself—at five with pigtails, at eight with a ponytail, at ten with hair pruned to her chin—see herself in the hills above the village. Rushing through green and white, fleeing or pursuing, she could not be sure.

She knew she didn't want sleep to stop. Waking brought a dullness, a deadening she grated against. The baby's howl and Slone's voice too seemed to emanate from some other cabin, from some other season in her mind.

The midnight impulses began then: standing naked at the window, motionless before a winter dark punctured by moon. Her hand on the glass as if trying to press through it.

Months tarried on in this manner before she began a partial exit from this place, that suspension between living and something else. The first day she was alone with her child she fought an urge to toss him into the fire. She was convinced that his birth meant the death of her.

IX

In the heated hangar at the mining camp, Slone packed his gear into the innkeeper's truck. He checked to make sure the tire chains were tight, filled the tank with fuel from a can, then loaded the can into the hatch.

Medora's red Blazer sat beside it, pocked and dulled beneath a solitary bulb dangling from a chain. Slone searched her truck, under the seats and floor mats, in the ashtray and glove box. Both back seats were folded down. He knew she'd slept here on her way to the mining camp and he ran his nose along the carpet, trying to smell hint of her.

Leaning against the truck, he smoked and watched the gray pall waft up and cohere inside the bowl of the bulb's metal shade. The hunter's blood remained flecked across the toe of his boot. He slid open the hangar's entrance and stood looking beyond his breath at this castaway place, then got in the truck to leave.

In the headlamps just outside the hangar he saw her, the innkeeper in untied boots and eyeglasses, in a nightgown under a woolen overcoat with no hood. Her hair wild, rifle aimed at the windshield, her face like a starved convict. The first shot punctured the glass to the left of his head. He swerved to miss her, instinctively ducked over the gearshift, the night a dark mass beyond the reach of the truck's high beams.

The shots came fast now into the truck, into the side windows and doors. He stretched for the pistol grip of the shotgun in the passenger's footwell but could not grasp it. The front axle scraped over a drift of hardened snow and the grille scraped against a mound of cinder block beneath a tarpaulin tied by rope.

When he righted the truck and spun she was no longer there, but he did not slow. The shot entered from the left dark, just behind him, through the window and seat and into his shoulder blade. A spasm jagged into his neck. The singe of lead, the sudden pressure in his abdomen, the need to urinate.

Lamps were beginning to burn again inside these shoddy homes, a floodlight now in glare from the high gable of the inn. The silhouettes of men and barrels, their hollers at him. More rifle rounds into the rear of the truck. He sped slipping on the rutted street to the access road at the far end of the camp, and in the dark he found the path back toward Keelut.

* * *

Hours later he halted at a junction in the wilderness. To his right was a snow-canopied path like a portal, one that would in several more miles open to the road north of town. He knew where he was now. At thirteen years old he and Cheeon had stolen his father's raised pickup and four-wheeled down this hidden byway, so muddied from spring's thaw. The mud sprayed out from the tires in billows, spattered the truck end to end, the wipers waving on high, two boys high-fiving in glee.

He paused now and lifted his clothes to see the blood pooled at the waistband of his thermals and pants. His shirt was fused to the skin of his back. He stood in snow to his shins and relieved himself there, his face aimed at a sky unseen and speckled with flakes, his mouth open for the gelid air. The wind wheezed through skeletal boles and branches with snow atop like icing. Then the wind fled west and there came a heavy quiet.

He scooped a plastic jug through untouched snow and set it on the dashboard heater to melt. After he drank he scooped more snow, every bit as thirsty as he'd been in the desert. And he listened to the quiet. In this land everything listened. The wilderness within and without. His father had told him that wolves can hear one another across three miles.

They can hear each other howl? he asked.

And his father said, *No, they can hear each other breathe.*

* * *

Shan Martin's place was south toward Keelut, twenty miles outside town, a fuel station, garage, and motel, nothing more. South the road connected to town and the highways, and north it led loggers, hunters, and fishermen farther into the bush. Shan and his father had left Keelut eleven years ago to run this business, for three hundred miles the last access to a bed or fixed transmission.

Slone arrived near ten p.m. and saw the two-bay garage lit inside, heard a radio singing. Through pulled drapes the motel rooms flickered with television light. In the lot sat a Mack semi, pickups salt-stained from highways, disabled cars cloaked in snow, a camouflaged four-wheeler with a frozen deer roped to a rack, its tongue in loll, eyes still looking.

Through a fogged window of the bay door he saw Shan smoking beneath the hood of a Jeep with knobby tires. He entered through the side door, entered into the wall of warmth, and said Shan's name. When Shan turned it took him several seconds to say anything, and then "Jesus Christ" was all he could utter.

Slone smelled grease and oil, the rubber of new tires. The radio gurgled an awful noise, an anthem for cowhands. Eviscerated trucks, orphaned engine parts everywhere. A new Polaris snow machine strapped to a trailer, plastic gas cans strapped behind it. The orange warmth came from a radiant heater overhead. Hung crookedly above the workbench was a year-old calendar with a half-nude model astride a motorcycle.

Shan was rounder, shorter now than when Slone had last seen him, years ago. A shaved head, tattoo of something behind his ear—a spider. Silver rings on every finger.

"Jesus Christ," Shan said, clicking off the radio. "Vernon Slone."

"One of those is right. I need your help."

"Christ, Vern. You're hurt?"

"I need you to get Cheeon for me."

"Cheeon? Jesus, where've you been, Vern?" He crushed his filter into a can full of them, then took up a stained newspaper from the workbench. "A trucker brought this paper through this morning."

He showed Slone the headline, Cheeon's photo there beneath it. Slone could remember the afternoon this photo was taken by Cheeon's wife. The afternoon they'd returned from the first big caribou hunt, August three years ago. Cheeon wearing a full beard then, his hair short and spiked, the rifle strapped aslant his torso. Flannel shirt damp with caribou blood, knife in his belt. In the original photo Slone was standing right there beside Cheeon but the newspaper had cropped him out of existence.

"Good ole Cheeon caused a real bloodbath back home," Shan told him. "I'm real sorry, man, I know you boys were tight."

Slone skimmed the sentences. He could not focus on them but understood the story they told.

"Them cops came looking for him and he just wasn't having any of it," Shan said. "Cheeon never did like them cops."

Slone needed to sit, but there was nowhere. He squatted with elbows on his knees, and between his boots examined a shape greased into the concrete floor—the shape of a running wolf. He stood then and took the cigarette and mug of coffee from Shan. For many minutes neither spoke, Shan shifting from foot to foot, suddenly interested in the grime stuck under his fingernails.

"You're shot?" Shan said.

Slone nodded with the coffee.

"Christ, Vern. Your upper back there?"

He was beginning not to feel the lead in his shoulder blade. He knew this was the start of not feeling his arm. A bullet aims to make a man aware of his body and then it aims to make him forget.

"Who shot you?"

"A woman."

"Shit, who ain't been shot by a woman?"

They finished their cigarettes in silence.

"They're looking for you, Vern. Medora too. They got rewards. Cops were here a week ago, I guess, or ten days ago, asking if she'd been through, for gas or anything else. What-all in the name of Jesus happened to that village?"

"Nothing in his name. Some things in the name of the other. I need your help."

Shan felt his shaved scalp, scratched at his ears. His forearm tattoo was now just a splotch of purple melanoma.

"Help how?" he said. "Because, shit, man, you're in this mess pretty deep, far as I can see it."

"I need this bullet out."

"Yeah, well, I thought that's what you were gonna say."

Slone did not move his eyes from him.

"Well, Christ, Vern. We grew up together, I haven't forgot it. I'm sorry as shit about your boy, I am. But I've got trouble enough my own self, with the cops too. And with my ex-wife. You remember Darcy?"

"You're gonna help me, Shan. That's what's happening now. That and nothing else."

"Jesus, Vernon."

Slone moved the handgun from the small of his back to the front of his pants, behind the belt buckle.

"I'd hate to remind you," he said. "Remind you that Cheeon and me were the ones who dug your mother's grave that summer. When your pop and you were too bad off to do it."

"Shit, man, I haven't forgot that. My pop's dead now, ya know. He died last year."

"Lots of people are dead now. And lots more will join them. Do you understand what I'm saying to you, Shan?"

They left the garage then and hauled Slone's duffel bags from the truck to a vacant room. Shan turned the heat high, then with scissors cut the shirt from Slone's back.

"Jesus, Vernon. What round made this hole, a .223, someone's Bushmaster? What's a nice lady doing with this rifle?"

"She ain't so nice."

"Must've gone through some shit before it found you, or else the thing'd be in your lung or heart right about now."

"The window and the seat."

"Damn lucky. Don't look like it hit anything important. It's not that deep, far as I can see."

"It's in the bone. You have to pull it."

"We gotta clean it first. We need vodka for this. Wait here."

"I don't need vodka."

"For me, man, I need it. Shit."

Slone checked the shotgun and slid it beneath a pillow, then put a rifle in the bathroom, another behind the door. He filled the pistol's clip and watched for Shan through a tweed curtain. Shan soon returned with a bag of clean clothes and a prescription of painkillers, rattling them in the bottle for Slone to see.

"These babies are why I'm in trouble with the cops, man, these here. You can't get this shit anymore. They're practically heroin pills. Here, take one now, because this ain't gonna feel too pretty at all."

He downed a pill with vodka as Shan stood at the sink and scrubbed the engine filth from his hands with a wire sponge and turpentine. Slone emptied his bags onto the bed for the peroxide, the needle-nose pliers, the razors, sewing kit, bandages, fishing line. Hunched at the edge of the bed, he held the pliers in the flame of a barbecue lighter. Shan unscrewed the shade from the lamp for better light, then laved Slone's upper back, the peroxide like an ember on the wound.

"Christ, sons of bitches sure like shooting at you, Vernon. What're these two scabs here, in your neck and shoulder here? You get these over there, where you were?"

Slone said nothing. They both drank again from the bottle and Slone winced against the burn of booze. Through the wafer wall he could hear the TV in the next room—a laugh track, a man's words about someone's wife not satisfying her husband, more laughter.

"I used to look for you on the news," Shan said. "Whenever there was a news report from there, about soldiers or whatever. But I never saw you. I thought I did one time, but it wasn't you."

"We used to look for you too. Cheeon and me. Whenever we were in town. But we never saw you either. After you left, we never saw you again."

"I never got into town much," Shan said. "Still don't."

"Nor back home much either."

Slone kept the pliers in the flame until they began to shift color and he felt the heat in the rubber handle.

"Those things gonna be long enough, man? I got longer ones in the garage, good ones."

"The longer you wait, the sooner it's infected. Pull it," and he handed him the pliers over his shoulder.

"You feel that pill yet?"

"I feel the bullet."

"Yeah, I would too. You want something to bite on? A belt maybe? Isn't that what they always use? A belt or a bullet? Though I'm guessing you don't even wanna look at another bullet right now."

"Pull it."

Slone sweated from his armpits and forehead as the pain knifed up to his neck, into his eyes, then a wider pain lashed down through his intestines and groin. His tears dripped onto the knees of his jeans. Shan grunted, trying to grasp the lead. "Stubborn son of a bitch," he said, and Slone could feel the blood spilling fast now along his back, could hear the grind of pliers on lead and bone. Saliva seeped, then spilled from his lips and chin. Twice he fought back the migraines of a fainting blackness.

"Jesus, stop bleeding, Vern, would ya? I can't see shit in all this mess you're making."

He poured vodka to rinse away the blood and then drank

from the bottle. Slone's pants were pink in places, damp red in others. Shan handed him the bottle for his own gulp and then began grasping again. His mumbling sounded to Slone like the mocking prayers of a comic.

"You gotta move closer into this light, Vernon. I simply cannot see shit here, man."

Shan dragged heavily on a cigarette as he leaned on the wall and mopped sweat from his face with a towel. Slone moved down the mattress and bent to hug his knees, to curve his upper back, the wound ripping, bleeding more. Shan put his cigarette into Slone's mouth and doused the wound with peroxide this time. He gave Slone a minute to smoke, to breathe again. To find some brace against this. Slone focused on the boot-stained carpet and felt the liquid spill from his shoulders and nape.

"Pull it," he said.

He was only half conscious when minutes later Shan withdrew the lead and showed it to him in the teeth of the pliers, grinning as if he'd hooked a halibut. From the pill and drink and pain Slone fell sideways onto the bed in a shallow dark as Shan worked fast to sluice the wound once more, to cross-stitch it closed with a beading needle and fishing line. Slone woke fully and asked if the round had fragmented.

"Negative," Shan said. "I got it all."

"You have to sew down through all seven skin layers."

"I'm way ahead of ya, Vernon, just lay there. Jesus, you act like this is the first bullet I ever pulled from a man. I had to pull that .22 round from Cheeon's calf when we were nine or ten. You shot your good buddy aiming for a rabbit. You started off a pretty bad shot, Vern. I been told you got better, though. Lay still."

The TV in the adjacent room was off now. They heard the couple there, the unoiled bedframe, uneven squeals that sounded half animal.

"How about that?" Shan said. "Good ole Roger is having a time with a rent-a-gal from town. Sorry for the walls. My pop cut corners where he could. They're nothing but a sheet of plasterboard on each side, no insulation even. Just enough studs to hold them up. You want another pill, Vern?"

But he was gone again in that depthless dark. Aware of the room and the hurt. But unmoored, skimming somewhere without human sound or any verge he could see. Just the purl of a streamlet somewhere beneath him.

Shan bandaged the spot, trussed it tight, then wedged off Slone's boots, helped to clothe him anew, wrap him in quilts that smelled of stale cold. He left with Slone's bloodied clothes to burn them in the furnace. In his partial darkness Slone felt for the shotgun on the pillow, felt into his coat pocket for the T-shirt that still held the scent of his son.

Shan returned minutes later holding a spoon and steaming tin pot. He sat on the bed near Slone.

"Sit up, man. You gotta have soup, Vernon. I'll help ya."

"Soup."

"Hell yes, soup. You know of anything soup can't fix? You need to eat some soup."

"What kind is it?"

"Vernon Slone. I just pulled a bullet from your back and every cop around is hunting you and you wanna know what *kind* of goddamn soup it is? It's Campbell's chicken soup. You know of a better soup than that?"

"I like tomato."

"*I like tomato*. Jesus Christ, you are something. Eat this soup, man."

* * *

In his sleep, inhaling his boy's T-shirt, Slone remembered it:

A tardy cold that autumn, the mornings finally below freezing in late October. Slone and Medora sixteen years old, setting out at six a.m. hand in hand through the hills outside Keelut. Plodding over footpaths they've known since childhood, miles down into the dale, across it to where the screes and crags slope up sharply from the plain. Avenues through cities of rock, scattered pine, and tufts of short spruce seen by only a dozen eyes before.

They wear packs with sandwiches and water, towels and candles. Every twenty minutes they rest to see the scape beyond. They kiss there against cliffs, soft at first and then harder. They touch conifer cones like infant pineapples that have shaken off rain. Two hours in and the temp has risen enough for them to remove their coats, to trek in sweaters and hats. At last they squeeze through crevices in the shadow-stroked crags, then track around to the cave, the steam exhaling from its entrance.

"Is that the one?" he asks her.

"Yes, that's it, hurry," she says, and smiling she pulls him along, up and around the rock-ribbed path to the cave.

Standing at the entrance on the slanted table of shale, with the sun strong at their backs now, they can see down into the hot spring. Steam in a steady hover on the surface of lucent water. She bounds smoothly over rocks into the heat of the cave, down to the rim of the pool. He follows her in. They erect candles in cracks around the pool, the steam aglow in a dozen small flames.

Their bodies are damp with sweat beneath their clothes. They strip bare, smiling at one another, Slone stiff already at the sight of her breasts in full weight, her blond patch of hair. Her velvet tongue tastes scantly of sugar. An inner writhing of excitement and need, at her touch a threshing all through him.

Her hand pumps him slowly there in the steam at the edge of the pool as they sit with their shins submerged. His fingers are gentle in her wet, his mouth on her breast, the skin of it almost liquid in its softness.

They enter the spring, its heat a whip on them at first, she in his arms as they spin laughing through the pool, as they go under together and hold, hold their breath, holding one another. When the heat swells they ascend to the mouth of the cave for October air to cool them. In the sun her blond nakedness seems the source of light, for an instant a halo about her matted crown.

This is a vision he will die with. The jolts and twitches deep within him, his arms around her in this morning chill, her breasts cradled in his hands. Soon they return to the warmth of the steam.

On a tabletop of rock above the pool they unroll towels. They lie enlaced and sweating. He's far inside her now and she claws a fistful of his hair and draws his face down to hers so she can breathe into his mouth, whisper her love into his throat. His left hand is pinched in her right, fingers linked, locked. Her white skin has turned rose from this twofold heat, a rash fanning from her breasts to neck. He waits for her to quiver and tense and when he empties inside her they both go limp.

And when Slone woke at Shan Martin's place, he knew where Medora was.

X

From his motel room's window Core saw the weak sun between a dip in the range, its warmth nothing to the ferns of frost smeared on the glass. His sickness had finally gone during a medicated sleep of eighteen hours. He was hungry now for chocolate and cigarettes. With a mug of coffee from the motel's lobby, he smoked at the window of his room as the sun glumly ascended, ice particles suspended in the air like mists of glitter, the cold a living thing—a willful thing with mind and lungs. He spat gobs of hardened phlegm into the bushes of snow beneath him. The engine above was a Cessna with skis cutting its way eastward and north to taxi men to their hunt. He planned to shower and leave this place, leave for the city to see his daughter.

But on the television a local news program, a female reporter in the village of Keelut, the microphone clouded by her breath. Core could not find the remote to unmute the sound but he read in blue ribbons at the bottom of the screen all that Cheeon had done there. Photos of the men he'd gunned down, a panning shot of Keelut— the water tower, generator shack, sled dogs, rows of cabins, those hills looming above. Another reporter at the morgue in town, shots of the parking lot behind it, Donald Marium being interviewed, looking bothered by the microphone so close to his mouth. More photos, the two cops Core remembered from the morgue, the coroner, the words "Vernon Slone," and Core felt an unsnapping just below his chest.

In the shower he leaned against the tiled wall, the overhot stream on his scalp, hair long enough to touch his mouth. He felt filthy from days of illness, filthier still after seeing all Cheeon and Slone had done. He'd packed a towel in the space under the door of the bathroom and the steam swelled there around him. The water off now, he sat holding himself in the tub, addled by a dread he fought to understand, newly disgusted by his body hair. He could recall Medora Slone scrubbing herself in the tub, how he'd peeked on the night he arrived in Keelut. He reached for the razor in his bag, ran the faucet, and with a circle of motel soap he spent the next hour shaving his body, unbothered by the many nicks that dripped blood in the water.

When he finally rose he wiped the mirror clear, and with scissors he clipped away his beard and hair, sweating still. Soon the sink filled with wet clumps of white. He shaved his face, his throat. The exposed skin felt bloomed, seemed to exhale after decades of held breath. He stood studying himself for a long while and for a moment he recognized the new father he'd been at twenty-five.

A red square flashed on the telephone but he was hesitant to hear whatever news this message brought. Perhaps his daughter, his wife, someone calling him to return home. But no one knew he was here. He sat on the unmade bed and looked at the pulse of light. It was Marium's voice saying he needed to meet, his office number, his cell. When Core dressed, his newly shaven body was cool and naked-feeling beneath his clothes, sensitive, strangely alive against flannel and denim. The sensation felt like a secret.

When he opened the door to get more coffee, a cop in a snowsuit was standing there. "Don Marium sent me to get you, Mr. Core."

"I just got his message, yes."

"He's in Keelut now. He wants us there."

"Yes," Core said, "I'll go to the village."

"I can drive you."

"I know the way," Core said. "I've been there before."

"Let me drive you," the cop said. "I know Don's looking to talk with you," and Core was irked by the way he'd said it.

* * *

An eighty-minute crawl to Keelut, half that time behind a weather-wrecked snowplow fanning salt and sand across the blacktop, the cop not eager to speak and Core glad for the quiet. He read the paper, articles about the Slones, about Cheeon, this village. A foot of new snow mantled the land, undulating up into the hills, into granite rock faces. Marium was there at the entrance to Keelut, his truck pointed at the Slones' cabin.

He waved through the windshield for Core, the cop walked off into the village, and Core joined Marium in the cab of the truck, the air burdened with the scent of coffee and smoke.

"Took me a sec to recognize you without the beard," Marium said.

Core stomped snow from his boots and shut the door.

"You got my message?"

"I did," Core said.

"I was surprised to see your truck still at the motel this morning. I thought you'd've got the hell out of here already. It's been over two weeks. Not had your fill of us yet?"

"I guess not. I've been sick. I'm two days behind on everything, I'm sorry."

Marium poured coffee from a bulletlike metallic thermos and passed a paper cup to Core. From beneath his seat he retrieved a fifth of whiskey and added a shot to his own coffee. Core reached over his cup for the same. He bit from a chocolate bar and started a cigarette with Marium's lighter.

"What did you need to speak with me about?" Core asked.

"Just trying to get all this figured out, Mr. Core. This mess we have here."

"I just saw what happened. I saw you on the news. You killed that man? Cheeon?"

Marium said nothing. His face did not change.

"How's a person do that?" Core said. "What Cheeon did here?"

"I was hoping you'd tell me that."

"Me? How would I know that?"

Marium looked at him through the steam of his coffee.

"If you corner an animal he'll try to claw his way out," Core said. "But that's not what happened here."

No animal, Core knew, does what Cheeon did. What Slone did at the morgue.

"I read some of your book last night," Marium said. "The one about wolves that Medora Slone had? I forget the title. Good book, though, the part I read."

"Why'd you want to read that?"

"I was hoping to learn something about Medora Slone." He paused. "Was hoping to learn something about you too, Mr. Core."

"Learn what?"

"Why she asked you to come here."

"And did you learn that?"

"Nope. Didn't learn a thing. Zip. I saw that wolves remind me of some bastards I know."

"That's unfair to wolves," Core said. "They have a logic some of us could use more of."

Marium looked at him over the top of his cup. "So I need to jog your memory, Mr. Core."

"How so?"

"You're the last one to see Medora Slone. Last one to talk to her. You found that boy. And right now I'm wondering why you're still here."

Core looked away to consider the hills, knowing he had no believable answer as to why he had not left this place. Because he'd been dreaming of Medora Slone. Because he'd been ruptured since finding the boy. Because he had little to return to. Because he was beginning to fear that man belongs neither in civilization nor nature—because we are aberrations between two states of being.

"I told you everything I know," Core said.

"Why are you still here?"

"You suspect me?"

"I'm just asking. It's my job to ask."

"I told you everything I know."

"I'm hoping you can tell me just a little more. That woman contacted you because she thought you'd understand her."

"That woman contacted me because she wanted me to find the boy," Core said.

"And that's my question, Mr. Core. Why you? Why a total stranger?"

"I don't know why me. She found my book on wolves. What are you implying here?"

"I'm not implying anything. I'm just stating what happened. A woman kills her boy and writes a complete stranger to come go on a wild wolf chase and then find the boy in a root cellar. Explain that, please."

"You asked me these questions two weeks ago."

"And I'm asking them again, fourteen bodies later."

Core felt grateful for the smoke hanging there between them like a curtain. He recalled Medora's body next to his on the sofa, the vision of her in the tub.

"Nothing happens here in a way that makes any sense," Core said. "You told me that yourself."

"That's not exactly what I said. What I'm saying now, Mr. Core, is that Medora Slone must have mentioned something to you, something that might tell me where she could be right now. Because if we want to get this thing figured out, we better find her before her husband does."

"Is that why Slone killed those cops at the morgue?"

Marium stubbed out his cigarette in the ashtray, then looked at the Slones' cabin. "He couldn't take the chance of us finding his wife before he did. That's my view of it. So they wouldn't take her to where he couldn't get at her."

"And the coroner too, why?"

"To get the boy's body," he said, pouring more coffee for himself and Core. "Or else he's just evil. It's not as uncommon as you might think."

Evil is a distortion of love—Core couldn't remember who said it or when, and didn't know how it helped explain what was upon them now.

"Slone let you drive away from the morgue that night," Marium said, lighting a new cigarette. "He let you go. Why would he do that? The wife calls you here, the husband lets you live. Why?"

Two village boys, eleven years old, padded in fur and face masks, blared by on a snow machine that sounded like a chain saw. Villagers shoveled pathways around their cabins. With their faces pressed deep into hoods, toddlers stood nearly immobile in moose-hide suits. Every few minutes someone stopped to stare at the men in the truck but did not raise a hand of welcome. The sun was nowhere. Core cracked the window another inch, felt the air move in his stomach.

"Are you gonna answer my question, please? Why did Slone let you drive away that night?"

"He wants a witness," Core said.

"A witness to what?"

"To this story he's telling."

"This story he's telling, okay. And Medora, she wants a witness too? That makes you the chosen storyteller, Mr. Core. Please explain that."

"How can I explain this?"

"Vernon Slone is a man and every man is explainable."

"What kind of man does this?" and he nodded out the window at the village, as if all of Keelut were the direful work of one person.

"The human kind," Marium said. "You should get a grip on that and you won't be so surprised all the time."

The human kind, Core thought, distressed in his new wavering between words, between *animal* and *human*, in this place where one world grated against the other. They sipped their coffees through silence, the wind-roused snow like mist against the glass. Core felt hungry for the first time today. Marium pressed on the radio, turned through the stations, searching, Core thought, for a weather report, for some fact he could understand. He didn't find anything he wanted and pressed it off.

"You didn't answer my question, Mr. Core."

"Which?"

"Why are you still here?"

"Because I'm trying to understand this thing, just like you," Core said. "I'm telling you everything I know. I'm trying to help. You should be talking to the people of this village, not me."

"These people will tell us nothing," Marium said. "They have their own laws. Or they think they do. They think the whole world is their enemy."

"They're your people, aren't they?"

"They sure as hell don't think so. And they're probably right. Just because you're from this region, that doesn't make you part of the blood of this village. Besides, as long as I have this job I'm their enemy."

"Slone killed that old woman here?" Core asked.

"I think so. It wasn't Cheeon, not his style. These people took her body. That's what I mean. They have their own laws."

"Did you find the boy's body?"

"Nope, not his either. You can't look anywhere now. Every eight hours new fall covers whatever there is to find."

"What about Slone's parents? Or Medora's? Has anyone talked to them? I imagine they can help you more than I can."

"Slone's father has been dead awhile," Marium said. "I'm not sure how. I don't know anything about his mother, never met her. I believe I've met Medora's mother in town, years ago. Very blond hair and white-white skin. Strange-looking woman, her mother.

Her father disappeared on a fishing trip. Someone told me that.
Went to sea and never came back. But I don't know that for sure."

"You've got to find out more about them."

"It's damn near impossible to know anything about these people, Mr. Core. That's the way they want it. Why they live here. Why
they stay. Everything you hear, you hear second- or third-hand and
you never know how much of it is true. These people don't come
into town all that often. And when they do, they keep to themselves."

"Still, someone should talk to the parents."

"We tried. The Feds tried. I just tried again half an hour ago. I
have a man out there trying again. No one here will tell you a damn
thing. These homes you see"—he pointed with his cigarette—"they
aren't listed in any phone book. These people don't have a paper
trail like you and me."

"There have to be records somewhere," Core said.

"You still haven't figured out where you are, have you?"

It occurred to Core then that his inability to comprehend this
place and its people—their refusal to be known—was part of the
reason he'd remained. He flicked his filter from the window, lit
another, then aimed two dashboard vents at his body. He shook
against a chill and reclined with his cup.

"So I'm on my own here, Mr. Core. I just went through their
cabin again, looking for whatever I missed the first two times."

"You've got to check the hills," Core said.

"We've had planes looking from here to the border and they
haven't seen a goddamn thing. I took up my own plane yesterday
before dark and there's nothing to see except white. East, west,
north, south—nothing but white."

"You fly?"

"You better fly or know someone who does if you live out here or you won't be able to get anywhere when you need to. We don't have roads like you have roads."

"They didn't go west," Core said.

"And you know that how?"

"West is the city and then the sea, right?"

"Eventually. So?"

"So watch wolves long enough and you'll see what their territory means to them. The Slones have been in these hills since they were old enough to walk. They won't flee somewhere they don't know."

"Keep going."

"I've seen some of what's out there past those hills," Core said. "I know you have too. I could see that tundra. She could hide forever in her own backyard and none of you would ever find her."

"Slone would find her. Unless he's thinking that she'd never run to the most obvious place there is. But that's what I need to know, Mr. Core, if I'm wasting my damn time here, if these people are long gone by now, deep into Canada or getting a suntan on a beach somewhere."

"No, they're still here," Core said.

A topo map of the region lay on the seat between them. Core unfolded it and tried to study its multiple lines and shades, but the vastness it showed would not be breached.

"If the people of this village came across Medora, hiding out there, like you say, they wouldn't turn her in," Marium said. "Even as what she's become, she's still one of their own. All the blood here is bonded."

"What has she become?" Core said.

"I should be asking you that."

Core looked away again and reached for the chocolate in his coat.

"What has that woman become, Mr. Core?"

We are the most unnatural of all, he thought.

"A child is the mother's," he said. "Not the father's and not anybody else's. Always the mother's in a way we'll never understand. It's the same wherever you look out there, in nature. She was trying to fix something. Something was broken and she thought she was fixing it. Or saving him from something. Trying to, anyway. I don't know."

"Who destroys something to fix it? Tell me who does that please."

"It happens in medicine," Core said. "Chemotherapy does just that."

"Are we talking about medicine or people here?"

"What Medora did is the same as chemotherapy. Kill the boy in order to save him."

"Save him from what?"

"I don't know that," Core told him. "Don't you think I'd say it if I knew? I'm trying to know." He lit another cigarette, studied Marium's lighter, a Zippo made of mock snakeskin. "Saving him from Slone, maybe. From becoming what his father is. I don't know."

"Well, I'll agree with you on one thing, Mr. Core. What happened here is a cancer of some kind. And believe me, when this is all done, I'm going on vacation, taking my wife to the Caribbean or someplace, nothing but green water and hot sand."

"The Caribbean?"

"Hell yes the Caribbean. But right now we're in this snow, Mr.

Core. So I need you to replay your conversation with Medora Slone. Start from the start and tell me everything she said to you."

A young girl trudged before them in snow past her knees with a .22 rifle strapped slant across her caribou coat, face and hair lost in a hood and ruff, an unleashed husky before her exploding a path in great clouds of powder. Core knew she was a girl by her gait. How could it feel to be from this place, to have your every molecule formed by its rhythms? Medora Slone had told him that Keelut wasn't of the earth, and he'd puzzled over those words since then.

But no place is of the earth—every place is of itself, knows only itself. The Caribbean? A child there is as peculiar, as particular as this child before him trudging through snow. Medora Slone, he recalled, had told him that she looked at magazine pictures of green water and island sand and wondered about those places, about their reality—their reality that seemed to her like mystery. She told him this right there on the road in front of him, between those rows of cabins, when she showed him where the wolves had invaded this village. She told him that the only warmth and water she had now was the hot spring hidden in the crags past the valley. Her special place, she said. And again he thought of her in the tub that night as she scoured her skin with a brush, as she tried to get clean and could not. He felt his own clean-shaven body against his clothing.

"She said something to me," Core told Marium. "The night I got here. She mentioned a hot spring to me. And I think I saw what she was talking about, that morning when I looked for the wolves. I saw a spring out there."

"Why a hot spring? I'm not following."

"If she's out there," Core said, "she'd need water. She'd need to get warm. Maybe she couldn't build a fire, couldn't risk being seen from the air, I don't know."

"Okay. Lots of hidden springs out there, Mr. Core. Where is this one you saw?"

"About a three-hour walk northeast from here."

"What else?"

"She called it her special place," Core said. "That's all. I don't know what else."

"Her special place. A hot spring." He flattened the topo map on the seat between them. "Show me," he said. "We're here," and he uncapped a red pen with his teeth, marked a crooked X on Keelut.

"It would be here then," Core said, pointing. "Although I can't make sense of this map. How old is this thing?"

"That's okay," Marium said, refolding the map. "You don't have to make sense of it. You can show me yourself at sunup."

"I'm sorry?"

"You're gonna show me where this spring is, Mr. Core. We'll fly over at sunup. We can't take off now. It'll be dark in two hours, and we're still an hour drive from town."

"It was just something she mentioned to me. I'm not saying she's there. How would I know?"

"If I had better leads than that, I'd follow them, believe me. But I don't. So you're gonna show me."

"Shouldn't you take men with you?" Core asked. "Other cops, I mean? I can't help you out there."

"How many men you think fit in a Cessna? You and me will go, you'll show me this spring, and if we find anything, we'll come back for more men. You can stay at our place tonight."

"I have a motel," Core said.

"Stay with us, I insist," he said, smiling. "We have a spare room. And you'll like my wife. We'll have a home-cooked meal."

"Because you'd rather keep an eye on me, you mean."

"You're free to leave, Mr. Core, you probably know that. But you haven't left yet, you're still right here talking to me. You can be a witness, whatever you want to call it, but you're gonna show me this spring."

Through the windshield, through blurs of blown snow, they watched the young girl and husky get swallowed by hulking cones of covered spruce. Marium swigged from whiskey again and passed the bottle to Core.

* * *

In his double-bay garage, at six a.m., the sun still loath to bring its light, Shan Martin dialed Marium's office—he had the number memorized—and tried to get him on the phone. "You tell Marium to call me, tell him I have information about Vernon Slone. I saw which way he's going and I believe that reward money is mine. You tell Marium to call me."

He returned the phone above the workbench to a cradle blackened by years of oil and grease. On the radio a weather report complaining of more storms, snow from the north. He flattened a cigarette filter into a can and moved a truck's carburetor aside. On a square of aluminum he crushed a pain pill with a hammer, then with a putty knife scraped the residue from the head and chopped, plowed the powder into a line. With a rolled one-dollar bill he snorted half into one nostril and half into the other.

When Shan turned, he saw him there by the door in a wolf mask, the pistol-grip shotgun at his side like a cane. The sight of Slone in his garage made it suddenly hard to breathe.

"Jesus, Vernon? What are you doing? The hell you wearing, man? I thought you left." His peculiar new voice was a choked wobble.

Slone stepped toward him slowly. Shan inched back against the workbench.

"Is this Halloween, man? The fuck you wearing?"

Slone's boots made not a sound on the concrete floor.

"I thought you left. You come back for some pills? That wound must be killing you. I can get you more."

Just the breathing inside the mask.

"You all right, man? I was just talking to Darcy on the phone, she wants more money from me, you know women, it's always that way with them."

Slone stepped nearer still and Shan looked to the gun. "The hell you doing, Vernon?" Slone raised it to pump the first slug into the chamber—a sound metallic and final in the cuboid cold of the garage.

Cornered where the workbench met the cinder-block wall, his face a welter of anguish, Shan pitched wrenches and screwdrivers that bounced from the padding of Slone's coat and clanged to the floor. He shrank more into the corner, his face now coiled in a noiseless sob. When Slone reached him, he pressed the barrel up hard beneath Shan's sternum. In the muzzle of the mask a hollow wet breathing, those familiar eyes embedded above a lupine snarl.

Sniveled pleas, an appeal to their past. Excuses—what the divorce had done to him, his abysmal debt. An apology for this betrayal, a prayer with tears. The radio sound behind them, the weather report foretelling of this winter's reign.

The blast ripped up through Shan Martin's chest and out his throat and face in a vermillion flare, thrust him back into the cinder block before he slumped dead to Slone's feet, his face leaking teeth and pieces from where his mouth had been. Slone lifted a garage door, backed up his truck to the new snow machine strapped to a trailer, then attached the trailer to the truck's hitch . . . on the radio behind him the weatherman trying to explain arctic air, still in calm drone about what was coming.

XI

A snowplow scraped against asphalt at eight in the morning, shook the house when it hit the curb. Core woke to its head-lamps and racket—woke in the spare bedroom in Marium's home, the room that in eight months would belong to Marium's child. Nothing in this room now but a single bed and an ironing board, the iron unplugged on a green carpet. No dresser, not a chair. Walls bare, a washed-out cream. Before sleep he'd felt that familiar sense of being afield in an unfamiliar bed, a welcome trespass among the scent of strange laundry soap. Lying wrapped in the dark and straining to hear the sounds of the house and not to make a sound himself.

The night before, Marium's wife, Susan, had cooked a meal of burbot and rice in a kitchen with appliances much older than her. All evening at the table she observed Core with barely veiled suspicion. He tried to diffuse such discomfort with talk of children.

"What's it like to have a daughter?" Susan said.

"It's good, though I'm not the best man to ask about kids. I haven't been the father I planned on being."

"I hear no one is," she said.

"I was away a lot, more than I wanted to be." *And I'm still away now*, he thought.

"You were away to work, I'm guessing," Marium said. "To make money. That was for her."

"There are ways to make money that don't involve being apart from your family. I was younger than you by a bit. What are you, forty-three? You're wanting a boy, I'd bet."

"Sure I do." He looked to Susan. "But a girl is good too. And I'm forty-eight. A fogey like me having my first kid."

"Fogey?" Core said. "I'll trade with you."

Now in the dark of the morning Marium knocked twice on the door to the spare bedroom. Core was already dressed, trying to unearth his toothbrush from the bottom of a duffel bag.

"Sunup is ten-fourteen," Marium said. "We gotta get to the plane. You're right that Slone is still here. We got a call in last night from a mining camp north of here. Slone was there yesterday and there's a dead man to prove it. Plus a call in early this morning from one of Slone's old buddies. We gotta get to the plane."

"Shouldn't you go talk to those people? I can wait here."

"There aren't any clear roads to that mining camp now, but I got a guy going to interview Slone's buddy. We're going to find that hot spring behind Keelut, Mr. Core."

As they drove through town, Core saw shops alight in dull fluorescence, their storefront windows thick with frost, slow shapes inside like fishes beneath lake ice. Bags of sand and salt stacked on a pallet in front of the hardware store. Someone had long forgotten to take down a wind chime and it hung now before the grocer's like a birdcage of ice. Stray citizens passed on a sanded sidewalk, sacks of larder slung across their shoulders. The hands of the clock tower frozen to the wrong time. The temperature was twenty below.

Marium rushed into a diner and returned with egg sandwiches and coffee.

"We won't have more than two hours' air time after sunup," he said. "You get caught in a blizzard this time of year and you lose the horizon. Then you hit a mountain or the ground and never even know it. You know what day it is?"

"Friday," Core told him.

"It's the winter solstice. Longest night of the year."

"All the nights here feel pretty long to me," Core said.

"Tonight is eighteen hours and thirty-three minutes of darkness."

"What's that mean?"

"It means we have to get back before that dark begins to fall. Slone's buddy left a message at the station at six this morning, and if he's right that he just saw Slone heading somewhere, that means Slone's got a four-hour lead time on us."

"Do you think this friend is right about seeing Slone? I doubt the man would let himself be seen."

"Shan Martin is a thief and I never met a thief that wasn't a liar too, so I don't know. But if Slone came out of the bush then he must have needed something. Food or ammo, or maybe he's hurt. The woman at the mining camp told us she shot the shit out of his truck."

"Call him, then, this Shan Martin," Core said.

"I tried, he's not picking up. I got a guy going there."

The sun broke then over the range, orange-pink and frigid-looking.

"What's the weather say?" Core asked.

"Says clear for now. But this place doesn't play by weather rules. Denali makes its own weather."

"Mount McKinley, you're talking about?"

"Denali, please, Mr. Core. You forty-eighters should quit calling it McKinley. Denali is the weathermaker. I've seen six feet of snow fall from a sky that two hours before was all baby blue with a smiley-face sun. There're more lost planes in this state than there're lost kittens in a city."

When they approached the lake, the sky was beginning to bruise in maroon and blue, a dim amber east through trees. At the shoreline the ski plane was dressed in insulated covers on its engine, tail, and wings—a lava-colored Cessna incongruous against this vast white. Core helped Marium unfasten the covers, then with brooms they swept snow from the flanks of the plane, the air so stinging he wondered how machinery could be coaxed into motion. How metal didn't fracture, crack from so much cold.

Core took the caribou one-piece suit from his duffel bag and began dressing at the door of the plane.

"Fancy outfit you got there," Marium said, still sweeping snow from the wing. "Where does a guy get one of those?"

"This belongs to Vernon Slone," Core told him. "The boots too."

Marium stopped sweeping then. He watched Core button the suit. He looked either appalled or superstitious but said nothing.

The engine belched twice before catching, before the propeller would consent to a throaty fan. Core had expected the leather and metal odor of a vehicle but he smelled only the cold, an odor that was no odor at all. A cold that forced him to breathe through the nose. When he breathed through his mouth his throat seized up into a coughing fit.

"How's any engine start in this cold?"

"It shouldn't be this cold so soon in the season. And I don't know where all this snow's coming from in such cold. Snow needs moisture and there's no moisture now. Something's wrong with the weather, I don't know what. But overall this isn't really cold, Mr. Core. Wait till February. That'll be cold."

"As long as this plane stays up."

"This plane doesn't quit till forty below. Guys working up in the arctic? They leave their Cats running day and night, never shut them off 'cause they won't ever start again. But us here: twenty below is a lark."

"Some lark."

"Thirty below, you gotta be a little more careful. Forty below and you better make sure a fire is five minutes away. And fifty below, don't even leave the house. People on the outskirts of town, living in dry cabins? They'll walk out in fifty below, walk down to a creek bed to cut ice for water, thinking they'll be gone maybe twenty minutes, so they don't dress right, and they never come back. Freeze solid right where they stand."

They waited for the engine to warm. The crown of sun crested distant trees, and all along the lakeshore wooded acreage breathed in snow. Through a break in the wood Core saw a large home, too many windows for a day this cold, its chimney awake with smoke. A kind of madness to live here, in this land that merged weather and flesh, that didn't let you forget.

He recalled reading accounts of those almost frozen to death in the arctic: first the lassitude, then the slurring of thoughts, memories in confusion, and then just before death you forget the freeze, a warmth spreads through the blood before your organs quit. As long as you feel the cold you're not about to die. Core could not remember being colder.

The last time he'd been in a plane this small he was twenty years old, being flown to pass twelve days in the remotest north of Minnesota. That was a winterscape like this one, limned with snow and ice, in the sun a crush of bright. The weather, he remembered, was like this—it had its own language, its own grammar of invigoration and hurt, but he was young then and welcomed it.

A plane floats on air as a boat floats on water. A friend from high school who became a Navy pilot had once told him this, but he could not understand the sense of it, the physics that performed the feat. Many tons of metal midair always seemed to him a supernatural act.

The cockpit warmed quickly. In the headset Marium's voice sounded less severe. The anticipation of flight lent it a lightness it lacked elsewhere. The skis upset snow in trailing mists as the plane sped to takeoff—white birch in easy blur along the lakeshore—and when they lifted it was not with thrust but a seamlessness he did not expect. The skis were so waxen along the snow of the lake that at first he did not even realize they were airborne, not until he turned to see the sinking spruce and birch, the lake falling away from them by feet.

Eastward from the lake he saw the sun fleshing pink all the white below it. Denali loomed to their left and looked not of this world. Beyond town were scattered homes, then broad fields etched with the day-old harrows of snow machines, mostly covered by new fall. Behind them slate clouds like fungus, storms hidden within. Minutes later a rolling whiteness, drifts of snow like waves from this height, ripples across a plain that then erupted into hills, into swells of snow. The marvel of this land cloyed with white. It seemed to Core a miracle it should ever have been discovered, ever have allowed itself to be trod on.

In twenty minutes Marium pointed as they came upon Keelut. "Tell me what we're looking for now," he said.

"Northeast," Core told him. "That valley there past the village, over those hills. You can tell the hot spring because it's the only spot down in the side of the rock that isn't covered in snow. Aim for those bluffs there off the plain."

"You see those there below us? Those tracks in the plain where the trees stop? Those are new snow machine tracks."

"Those could be anybody's," Core said.

"They're somebody's, that's for sure."

Soon they neared an oval of hills, uneven cliffs with a pan between, a rift inside a fort of crags. They passed low along hummocks, along corniced ridges. They looked for tracks in the snow of the escarpment. Core pointed to the steam exhaling thinly from a bald hollow in the brow of a crag, brassy rock sprouted from snow.

"That's it there," Core said. "See it? I don't see a truck or tracks. You can't be down there without making tracks to show it."

"It snowed last night. Not much, but enough to cover whatever tracks were there."

"I don't see anything," Core said.

"Let's look closer. I can set her down there between those hills. We've got a bit before those clouds catch us."

"You're landing here?"

"I'm a smooth lander, Mr. Core, don't worry."

They set down on a suede drag and circled back closer to the cliffs. Marium strapped the scoped Remington across his jacket and gave the field glasses to Core. Leaning against the aircraft they smoked and ate chocolate. In quiet they considered the crags, this rock forged epochs ago. The wind came in raspy blows and chafed snow from the wide face of the cliff. The day was gaunt, already half gone, and to the west of them the land looked laced to sky.

Marium passed Core charcoal heating pads. "Slip two of those into your bunny boots," he said. "And save two for your hands. Fingers and toes are the first to go out here. It's probably twenty degrees colder than it was when you were last out here. Probably more. Do you recognize where we are?"

"I came that way, through that break in the hills there. But I was on the other side of these crags. I can try to get us there."

Kicking through new snowfall on the talus, trudging over landslips and scree, they sought entrance through this rise of cliffs. They had to breathe sideways when the wind swiped from the plain. Core touched great polyps and pikes of ice on the rock walls, some clear as shellac, others opaque as bone, one like a waterfall on pause. For fifteen minutes they labored along the sloped perimeter of cliffs. Core stopped when he came to the wolf tracks stamped in the shallow felt of snow, tracks that padded from view around the bluff.

"How fresh are they?" Marium said.

"An hour or two, I'd say. Four of them. Adults. A hundred pounds apiece, give or take."

"Four of them. Where's the rest of the pack?" Marium unstrapped the rifle and bolted the first round, snow and beads of ice on his beard of mixed browns.

"Not far, I'd guess. Their den must be near here. Should we go back?"

"Let's look a little farther," Marium said.

"We don't want to meet those wolves."

"Let's look a bit farther. If we see sign of anything we'll turn back."

More hard walking along the scree and gusts turned to gale, air of solid snow swept quick from the plain. Marium pointed to a cavity in the spur of the crag and they moved up into it. They sat on rocks free from the whited wind. They smoked, watching walls of snow blow by them.

"Can we take off in this?" Core said.

"Not in this. It'll pass soon. This isn't whiteout. You'll know whiteout when it comes because you won't believe it."

And then: "When I was a kid my mother told me about an Eskimo woman who had to make half a day's journey from one village to another and midway she got caught in a blizzard. A heavy, blinding whiteout. She was carrying a bearskin to bring to the other village, and she burrowed a hole down into the snow, four or five feet deep, curled up in the bearskin and went to sleep. The blizzard roared for two days straight, and when it stopped, she woke up, crawled out, and walked on to where she was going."

"How's that possible?"

"She stayed dry. You get wet out here, you're dead. You ever read *Last of the Breed*, that book by Louis L'Amour?"

"No. But my father liked that one. It's one of the last things I remember about him. The paperback—I remember it was a thick blue paperback."

"Yeah, the cover shows Joe Mack running through the snow. There's a scene where Mack swims across the river in below-zero weather in Siberia, and then just keeps going, like he was in Honolulu or some goddamn place. If you get wet like that, in that temperature, and don't make a fire in five, six minutes tops, you're dead. That Eskimo woman survived because she stayed dry."

"And women are stronger than men," Core said. "You'll see how. You'll see in eight months."

"We gotta move to keep warm. Those charcoal pads working in your boots?"

"They're working."

The gale diminished and they walked on minutes more along the loins of the crag to a man-width slit, a path they squeezed into, free once more from wind, free to hear their breath. They coursed through to the rift inside the oval of cliffs, and across the pan they saw the spring exhaling its steam.

"How'd you spot this in here?" Marium said.

"I was up on the ridge at the far side, glassing the valley. It's an easy climb from that side. I should have taken us that way, I'm sorry."

They walked along against the wall of rock and Core stopped to glass the ridgeline. "There's movement up there."

"What movement?"

"I'm not sure," Core said. "Wolves maybe."

"Why would wolves be up on the ridge?"

"They can see better from there."

"See what better?"

"See us better," Core said.

"They climbed to the ridge to see us? Are you kidding?"

He passed the glasses to Marium. "There is no smarter hunter. Not out here. Do you see movement?"

"Nothing now," he said, and handed the glasses back to Core.

"Let's sit here until they move on."

"We can't sit long. We gotta move."

They sat on boulders and looked across the pan at steam rising from the spring and at the ridgeline above it. Core tried to start another cigarette but the lighter would not fire.

"It's too cold for that lighter to work right," Marium said. "The fluid is all gel. Take these," and he dug into his parka for a box of wood matches. "We can't sit long."

Core lifted the glasses and looked again at the ridgeline. And as he did a figure hove into view, stepped slowly at the crest, forty yards from them across the rift. A wolf for certain, he thought, and he said Marium's name. Both men stood then. Core trained the glasses on the ridgeline and saw the figure rise now full over the crest and stand on two legs against an iron sky.

Core instinctively reached for Marium's arm and then focused the glasses. What he saw did not fit: a man with the face of a wolf—pointed ears and an elongated black face in front of yellow hair. His bow was already drawn and steady by the time Core could see him in focus.

The rifle dropped into the snow at his feet. When he turned, Marium was against the rock face with the arrow through his throat, the tip poking through his nape, hands around the shaft as if he could keep it from doing more harm. The noise coming from his neck was a gurgled sigh, his teeth red and dripping. Core dove, grabbed on to Marium's legs at the knees, and tugged him down behind a berm of fallen rock just as another arrow smashed, sparked against the crag.

Blood pulsed from the shaft thick and almost black but in the snow made a shock of red. Core gnashed off a glove and drew the arrow from Marium's neck, but he was already still, his chest and throat already without sound, his lids closed and the front of his jacket stained through. Core lay on him, thinking to keep him from cold, his breath plugged in his breast. How odd that the groaning wind could breach the oval of crags, but then he listened again. The groaning was his.

XII

Core took up the rifle from the bloodied snow near Donald Marium's feet. From the berm of rock he aimed through the scope to where Slone had stood on the ridgeline with the bow—he knew it was Slone—but he was not there now. He lay again, low behind the berm, half the air clipped from him, looking at Marium fast turning to frost, his cheeks and lips now an identical ash, a rivulet of red from his mouth, pebbles of blood frozen in his beard.

Christmas was four days away and he would have this gift for Susan, the wife with child who had glared at him last night over dinner in her home. He was the invader, he knew. Messenger from the other world, taker of her husband. He wondered at the anguish of this place, all those snowed-over acres accountable to nothing.

He retreated with the rifle back through the cleft in the rock, and from the sheltered path he emerged again into an onrush of wind and snow. The wind pushed at him, groped against him, the snow like stones on his face.

Beneath his hood he unrolled his hat down into its face mask and pulled on goggles. Just then he heard the chorus of wolves behind the crags, their plaintive howling borne on the gale. He rushed along the talus to the level strip where the plane sat in its cherry paint behind webs of snow. This blizzard had come again quickly and he trudged through it aslant to keep the gusts from stealing his breath. Every few seconds he looked above to the ridge of the tallest crag and expected to spot Slone there with his bow drawn.

The door of the plane flapped in the gale. When he approached he saw the left engine cowling thrust open, hoses and wires hacked through, spark plugs stolen. In the cockpit he forced the door shut against the wind and tried to breathe. He saw the knife wounds through the instrument panel and radios. Wind nudged the plane, wailed around the windows and wings. He wanted to weep from cold. Moisture froze inside his nostrils. When his left eye wouldn't open he knew it was sealed with ice. He rubbed it frantically for fear of blindness, then cupped a wood match in his palm. He brought the flame near enough his face to inhale its heat.

The mind is the great poem of winter. He recalled those words but could not name the poet and could only guess now at what it meant—this scape identical to the mind, in moments knowable to itself. It touches the past, foretells the future. He worried that the plates, the fault lines beneath his own mind were now starting to shift, to cause a quake he could not stop. The mind's mountains, those cliffs to fall from. At a certain point this place obliterated all imagination. Like the sun, it refused to let you impose yourself upon it.

Out the cockpit window he tried to imagine the tundra beyond these crags, a breadth so barren now even wolves sought reprieve. Primitive man must have looked with horror upon such foreboding land. What doctrine of the soul would have saved them? They died without souls. He knew that in the earth, under this veil of snow and ice, there flourished spores of life blown here from the vacuum of space. How far below him did the earth's lava like blood surge under crust? *But we were not born to survive. Only to live.* He knew his thoughts were those of a dying man.

Marium's blood was stained like shards of glass on his jacket and gloves, droplets on his pants and in the laces of his boots. He imagined himself a mummy found in summer inside this plane, dead for two seasons, his gnarled body a warning to those who sought to trespass here. He thought of the phone call to his daughter, the news from an uncaring official, but when he summoned her face it was three years old, his daughter as a child before time took her from him.

In the cargo space behind the rear seat he found a canvas duffel bag, inside a first-aid kit, aerial map, hunting knife, rounds for the Remington rifle, a dog-eared paperback called *Prepare for Fatherhood*, and in a buttoned side pouch an unopened fifth of whiskey. He said Marium's name aloud and sat on the floor of the plane, between the seats, drinking from the bottle. Snow swarmed more against the windows. The whiskey heated him from within, reached all the way to his feet. He unearthed the chocolate from inside his overalls and lit his last cigarette, the cramped space of the plane filling with a smoke hued blue in the cold.

Winter solstice, he remembered then, Marium's words from that morning, eighteen hours of night. He could stay here, he knew. He could pass into a drunken sleep and simply stay. He could recline with this bottle and simply wait—wait for the cold to change to a deceiving warmth before the final dark.

* * *

He needed to move. A stiffness had begun spreading up his shins and into his hips, a creaking he could almost hear. A final sip from the whiskey bottle and he pocketed the hunting knife and rifle rounds, then stepped out from the plane. He made his hard way again into the gale, onto the rutted talus, around the bluff, the snow erected there in the air like walls, great windrows along the rock face. He fought through them to the spot where he and Marium had rested. The new footprints here were Slone's. At the spur of the crag the prints doubled back and Core turned with the rifle, terrified Slone was behind him.

And as he tried to reach the chasm on the east side of the crag, he turned every few seconds, expecting to spot Slone behind him along the rock face, blurred by snow. The footpath through the chasm was obscured by new fall atop crisps of hoar and snarled with loosed rock, but it was still and silent screened from the gale. He paused here at the head of the path to look back for Slone.

At the top of this path, canopied by rock, he knelt beneath a fluted cornice of snow with the rifle ready. Into this tall oval, away from the wind, snow floated as if part of a nativity. To his right fifty yards down lay Marium's brown boots jutting out from behind the berm.

He cross-shouldered the rifle and stepped out from the path onto boulders and flat shapes of shale, testing each foot down. At the bottom he hid behind a berm, and in the rifle's scope he saw the entrance of the spring, steam on black. Breathing, he waited. When he moved again he stayed close to the inner face of the cliff as he crept around to the rocks spilled like a bumped tongue from the mouth of the spring.

He ascended the ramp to the level swatch of shale at the mouth and crouched there with the rifle, aiming in as far as light would go. Beneath his boots the hardened dung of lynx or Dall sheep. To his right just inside, a fire pit circular and charred, beside it the toothpick bones of a ptarmigan, others from a snowshoe hare. The warmth of the spring wet his lungs and he rolled up his face mask and hunkered into the spring with hesitant steps.

By minutes his eyes adjusted to the weakling light and he saw down the slant of stone to the pool venting steam, beyond it crevices vanishing into earth. He squatted and watched with the rifle, listened to the cavern and inched in farther, glad for this hugging heat.

Ten yards from him in a corner of partial dark, atop the incline of flat rock, he saw her feet, new mukluks of moose hide where the light stopped stretching. Beside her against stone were a stack of blankets and cans of food, a rifle and lantern. He padded in farther toward the corner, the gun trained just above her feet, an anticipation in him like liquid that felt part fatal. She angled her shoulders and head from the shadows and then he saw her face. She was sitting on a sleeping bag leaned against the wall of stone, her cheeks sucked in from hunger, her eyes heavy in a way that spoke of either exhaustion or indifference.

Core said her name. His voice in this cave was an echoed noise he had not heard before. He kept the gun on her chest, squinted to see if she held a weapon, but her hands were folded at her waist. He asked if she was injured but she leaned her head back on the stone and considered him in what seemed boredom. Sweating now, he shed his gloves, peeled off the one-piece suit of caribou, and lay the rifle across it. He went to the paraffin lamp and lit the wick, her face warmed by the sheen of light. The girlish beauty he remembered, the white-blond hair. He asked again if she was injured and moved toward her with the lamp, stood before her, on the rounded stone walls and vault his lank shadow like ink.

"Medora," he said. "Medora Slone."

She would not or could not speak, had seemed to arrive at some place past words, a limbo between worlds where language failed—movement or no movement but never words.

"We have to leave. He's coming. He's behind me. He's coming for you."

She would not move and Core repeated, "He's coming."

Then in the lamplight her face changed, twisted, and from her neck and chest came a moan, a low caw of dread. Core turned and saw him there at the mouth of the cave, the silhouetted form of Vernon Slone in the wolf mask, standing before the flurried gray-white of day.

The arrow lanced through just beneath his collar, noiseless and smooth, no slap against the body, no impact on bone. The orange vanes of the arrow against his shirt, two feet of shaft jabbing out from his back. The sound he heard now was his own gasping as he leaned against stone, as he slid several feet to his side. He lay uneven on plates of shale, his mouth flushed with saliva that drooled over dry lips. A nausea now, this fear a vexed knowing of death.

For this he had come. For this he had remained.

Sideways on the stone, he sweated and bled watching Slone stalk into the cave with the bow. Core glanced to the rifle out of reach on the caribou suit, then listened to his own damp gasp and behind him to the muted whimpers of Medora Slone. A numbness was replacing the pain now, spreading from his neck and chest, down into his left arm and his fingers tipped with blood. He understood that he would be dead soon.

Slone stepped toward Medora. He dropped the bow and stood looking at her in the lamp-lit corner of the cave. She sobbed with no sound. Core thought he could hear Slone breathing inside the mask but the wheeze was the blood bubbled within his own breast.

Slone stopped at Medora's feet, his head tilted at her one way, then the other, as if trying to recognize her after thirteen months apart—after all she'd done. She wept and extended her arms to him, wanting end to this havoc. And he bent then with both hands clasped to her throat and hoisted her up, smashed her hard against the stone.

Core's voice, the shouts at Slone, would not come—they were pinned in his gullet beneath the blood. She gagged in Slone's grip, tried to kick free, then reached to lift the mask from his face. The mask dropped to the stone and she grabbed fistfuls of his hair and pulled his head to hers. When their faces hit he loosened his grip, loosened more, and found her lips. They breathed, groaned that way into one another's mouth, haled at one another's hair, their animal noises weaved with hurt, with the hunger born of separation.

They tore at their clothing with that hunger and Core saw them drop nude in a corner not breached by lamplight. He glimpsed her full breast and thigh before a shadow swallowed them. Heard a rapt keening he hadn't thought possible from a person. He almost recalled that splendor, almost remembered youth, his wife and daughter now crystal figurines in memory. He lay on stone fading, feeling himself rasp and wane and sweat, unable to summon the buried prayer he wanted.

In time a body emerged nude from the shadows and steam, into the lantern light, his blond beard stippled with dew, chin-length hair tangled and wet. He woke Core fully, startled him from his slow falling through layers of air. *You would not seek me if you had not found me.* He went to one knee to grab the shaft of the arrow at Core's upper back, then drew it through, yanked it clean, quick, but the pain spiked up from the wound and through Core's neck, into his teeth, the bones of his cheeks, reeling in ripples.

On the sleeve of Core's shirt Slone wiped the blood from the arrow and squatted there to consider him. Core could not make sense of Slone's face, could not ascertain the mysteries there. Behind him Medora stepped slowly from the dark, her matte flesh dappled with rash, an inch of semen slipping down her inner thigh. He shook from the cold of blood loss, the heat of this spring unable to warm him now. Medora draped the caribou suit over his torso and legs, tucked the hood around his throat, then knelt near Slone and reached for Core's hand. She seemed willing to comprehend Core's confusion and love. He nearly smiled.

Seeing their faces side by side, Core could notice the same dimpled chin and bumped nasal bridge, the identical ecru of their eyes. He knew his vision must be merging them, knew his mind was dying.

He looked at Slone. "The boots," he managed, though his throat and mouth were so dry with thirst he barely heard his own words.

Slone leaned in to him, squinted to show he didn't understand.

"The boots," Core said again, nodding to his own feet. "They're yours."

Slone looked to the boots Medora had lent Core for his hunting of the wolves, then looked back to Core with a partial grin, an expression that told him to keep the boots. He rose to go, and when Medora released Core's hand he once more felt his long falling.

They dressed and packed their provisions, packed the rifles and bow, the blankets and lantern. Core watched them between lengthy blinks. Before they left him in the dark and steam of the cave, Slone came to him once more, crouched to place a lit cigarette in Core's lips. With his left hand numbed and gummy in blood, Core struggled to dig out the chocolate from the wide bib of his overalls and then unpeeled the foil with his teeth.

He smoked on the taste of chocolate spiced with blood, and listened to them leave the spring, descend out of earshot until he was alone in the hush and dark. Where the day's ill gray light grazed the rock above him he saw his smoke fuse with steam, cohere into shapes whose meaning he could not divine. Such shapes: he would have liked to paint them. He remembered he'd been a painter. And he would have painted them with purpose, with the grace not given to him now.

Sorry not to be dying from an excess of whiskey and tobacco, he wished he'd allowed himself more pleasure these last thirty-five years. Other people were defective wells of pleasure. They sought pleasure of their own. They ripened or rotted away from you, left you bumbling. He was a white-haired man who'd invested in a future that forgot him. He saw distinctly now the faces of his father and mother—their youthful faces as new parents—but could not see their deaths because he was not there. Most of us get the deaths we've earned. Not Bailey Slone.

And then he was crawling on arms he could not feel, leaving red-brown hand marks on the ribbed ground of rock. He dragged himself to the mouth of the cave, half his body in the snow and failing light. On his elbows and belly he looked down into the pan. The Slones were crossing to the cleft in the rock. He collapsed then and rolled, first to his shoulder and flank and then to his back, his arms outstretched.

He could feel the flakes on his forehead and mouth, the chill seeping into his clothes. This cream sky had no layers, no divisions of cloud—he stared into a gauze without knowable start or finish, flakes coming from a fuzzed heaven.

The silhouettes on the ridgeline to his right were the wolves heeding him with abnormal calm, six of them waiting. How he admired their patience, their wisdom to wait. Before he dropped heavy through strata of varied black, he felt, for an instant, honored to give them this sustenance. He felt honored to lose the confines of his flesh, to let it give them life. And before he slept, he saw the boy standing behind the wolves—Bailey Slone, looking just as Core had found him in the root cellar, the strangle mark on his throat, his complexion the white of the dead, his eyes telling Core there was much to fear.

*　*　*

The four men who woke him wore goggled faces pressed far into the hoods of wolf-ruff parkas. They did not speak. Terrifying angels without wings. Behind their heads the padded sky had started to darken in purple casts, and it darkened more now as the men passed before it. With mittens they brushed a film of fallen snow from the top half of his body. One man propped him upright at the waist, while two others stretched and pulled the one-piece caribou suit onto him. Without the body-wide burn of cold and the pain of the arrow wound he guessed this was his death.

They wrapped him in a blanket—a shrouded corpse, he thought—and lifted him by the shoulders and feet, placed him on a pelt. They carried him down from the spring, into the pan. They had no haste—a funeral procession. As they reached the wall of rock Core could see beneath him the spot where Marium's body had been, the teeth-torn clothes and bone, the pink mess his innards had made, paw prints of blood. Core knew the wolves had feasted, but had spared him, though being spared had not been his wish.

Two sled-dog teams rested or nipped at one another in the snow. When the men came through the gap in the crags the ready dogs stood mindful. The snow had ebbed. In the east the full yellow moon shone through a rip in clouds. The men laid him on the bed slats of a dogsled. He felt himself being encased in the pelt with a husky who lay beside him—the clean cold scent of its fur, its wet nose on his mouth and chin.

They packed him and the husky against the stanchions with more pelts, his head on the brush bow, his face in the animal's neck, his body slowly imbued by the eighty-pound heat of the dog. Under him he felt the rough skidding of the runners on crusted snow, and then the smooth riding in fresh fall as the sleds mushed on toward moonlight.

Each time he dipped into a shallow sleep he expected the abyss, expected not to wake, not to rise. When he did, he once again felt the sled's motion, smelled the dog, heard the canine yelps just ahead of him. Each time he woke he had to learn anew that he was not dead. A jagged passage—one hour or two, he could not be sure, time had turned into a back-and-forth slosh of sand, his memory leaping over decades. The sleds arrived in the village of Keelut.

The men carried him into a cabin and left, left him in front of the fire with a huddle of short-sleeved women who unwrapped the blanket from his body and stripped him to the waist. The arrow wound had ceased bleeding, had dried front and back in dark caps. A woman brought a basin of warm water and rags. They stripped him full and washed him there on the floor before the fire, on a blue tarpaulin, lifted his head so he could drink from a squeeze bottle, and when the wounds were clean they daubed them with a pungent ointment that chilled before it stung. He saw a blond woman take up the caribou suit. She looked it over, sniffed it for scent, and Core could not comprehend what was happening.

With car-wash sponges they rinsed his lap and legs where blood clung in clotted naps. He lay aware of the water and air on his shrunken genitals, but he was unashamed. They dried him gently and then dressed him in clothing soft and old with mothball scent. The tenderness of the female hands on his chest and limbs took him close to weeping.

When had such loving hands touched him last? He was just then willing to die, again and again, to experience such affection, such saving as this. Before apathy had claimed him how often had he gone to the barber for just that reason? Not because his hair needed trimming but because those hands on his head were a confirmation that he was still here, still capable of knowing touch. No body massage ever felt as fine as a barber's delicate fingers.

They gave him more water from the bottle and then brought a cast-iron pot warmed in the fire, an acrid broth gamy and sweet. The blond woman fed him with a birch ladle, a woman near his age, it seemed—the mother of either Medora or Vernon Slone, he was sure.

He drank the broth while others held him upright. He could not shift his eyes from this woman who fed him because he saw that her face, by some witch's trick, was a mix of both Medora and Vernon Slone—the fine blond hair, the nose and chin, the yellow-brown eyes and oval ears. In this woman's still-lovely face he could behold both of the Slones. She was the mother of both. He recalled the matching faces of her daughter and son as they'd knelt beside him in the steam of the cave.

And before he let sleep drag him down into a wide pasture of night, he understood that this one woman above him, this woman caring enough to save him, was not just the source of both faces, but also, perhaps, the reason for the wolves.

* * *

When he woke the following morning in a hospital in town his daughter was there, sitting beside him in a wooden chair, wearing glasses he'd never noticed, a red sweater as if to welcome the holiday. Her smile signaled only the smallest relief. In the medicated fog of waking he believed for a minute that she was his wife thirty years ago. He glanced to the blanket then and felt his hand in her own.

She'd want to know all he'd witnessed. She'd want to hear the truth of these events. But he would have for her only a story—one that seemed to have happened half in dream, rent from the regular world he knew—and that story would wear the clothes of truth. Propped up in bed, he prepared himself for this tale. He searched for the beginning, and for the will to believe it.

XIII

They spent the remaining months of winter many miles from Keelut, in their father's sod igloo hidden in the taiga, an earthen grot he'd built when they were children for three-week hunting trips. They'd known about these crude outposts all their lives—many hunters in the village had built them for the winter hunt when the caribou migrated east. In the valley beyond the village their mother had left them backpacks of provisions, including a map with the location of their father's sod igloo circled in blue pen.

It had taken them an entire day to find it, in four-wheel drive on pathways until the truck was choked by snow, until they were forced to walk, carrying what they could. They dug for forty minutes through drifts to reach the entrance, the pine door that looked clawed at by grizzly. Once inside they found it dry, with a working stove, cut wood and kindling stacked beside it, steel drums packed with nonperishables made before their birth. That clean scent of frigid earth until Slone cleared the vent of snow and started the stove.

They saw at once that their father had stocked this lee with food for two seasons: Bisquick and beans, oatmeal and rice, noodles and raisins, powdered milk and coffee, dried peaches and apricots. In a different drum: medical kits, candles and matches, radio and batteries, tissue paper and snowshoe bindings, Coleman fuel and lantern wicks. The chocolate she'd devoured as a child and hadn't seen in years. Cartons of cigarettes. Sweaters, socks, long johns, overalls. Blankets, ammunition, books. A mattress hung by wire from the low ceiling to keep rodents away. With sugar and vanilla they could make ice cream of snow.

Perhaps, she thought, their father had prepared for this very day, the day when his twins would need this shelter—the day their otherness became known and they were forced to flee, to enact their exile from the world for sins they could not control. She hadn't seen their father's face in six years, since the evening before he slipped a shotgun barrel into his mouth and pressed the trigger with his toe, but she remembered it, could recall his cigarette scent, his voice always as rough, as stubbled as his appearance. This sod igloo meant that he'd loved her, she knew—meant that he'd loved them both, no matter their otherness.

They slept and ate and read, feasted on one another in the afternoon. She rebandaged the bullet wound in his upper back, applied ointment, pulled the stitching once it fully healed. For weeks they did little but lie naked beneath blankets as snow piled around them, exhausted in a way she'd never felt before, the stove too much heat for this small lee. He chopped more wood and hunted lynx, fox, rabbit, whatever he could find, but a famine was still on this land and he couldn't find much. He kept the rifles ready by the entrance, shotgun by the stove, handgun always in his belt. He told her what to do if ever he was out and she heard men coming through the thick. In six places around the perimeter he strung tripwire between trees, in front of the wire sharpened sticks in the snow to impale a man. One afternoon, hunting before dusk, they came upon a single-engine propeller plane suspended, mangled in the treetops, camouflaged in snow—one of the countless lost planes in this country. Lighter than her brother, always the better climber, she let him hoist her into the branches and she made her careful way to the plane above. Through the shattered glass she saw the bush pilot seat-belted in a bank of snow, just a wool-clad skeleton now, the headset still fastened to its skull. The propeller was smashed back into the engine from the impact, on the door black streaks from fire. The tail cracked and dangling, one wing snapped off, bent beneath the fuselage. She brushed snow from the other wing, tested her weight on it, and entered through the missing glass. Behind the seats several wood-slat crates of mail. The year stamped on the letters was 1968. She dropped a bag down to Slone—there was nothing in the plane they needed—and for two weeks that winter she read these letters, forgotten messages from worlds she tried to imagine, amazed by the varied handwriting of people who had long since moved on to other lives.

She read these lines aloud to Slone, dulled blue ink on peach-colored paper that still held a ghostly whiff of perfume, lines from Mary to Joseph that began, "Please don't you dare go to that jungle over there. There's no love in war and I have all this love for you waiting. You can dodge it, Joe. Just run, come here to me, stay with me, they'll never find you here."

* * *

Winter diminished and breakup came, spring a savior she thought hadn't remembered them. It was always that way, she knew. By the end of each March they always believed themselves forgotten by spring.

Slone dug a larger sod igloo into a wooded ridge near the rim of taiga, hidden from the ancient caribou trail and from the sky beneath the hemlock. Just ten feet from them in the forest no one could know they were there. She watched him work shirtless in moving shafts of sunlight, watched him dig high enough into the earth, above the water table, careful of proper drainage to keep them dry. She watched him frame the structure from spruce, make the notched posts and ridge beams, pound poles into the soil.

He built with tools others from the village had left for them in the valley—whipsaw and axe, hammer and mallet, shovel and pick, bag of nails and spikes, roll of plastic sheeting. She helped with saplings for the sod-block walls, with the pilings, helped cut and carry sod. She scraped clean the conifers for the roof. She learned how to fasten the beam joints with spikes. He taught her this with a patience that surprised her.

No windows. A rounded entrance of five feet. Together they carted the mattress and woodstove from their father's igloo, carted the goods their father had stored for them. They trekked to both of their vehicles, hidden in the hills two miles apart, and trekked back with the duffel bags of supplies they'd been unable to carry in winter.

They moved by starlight sometimes, whenever they'd noticed the same plane in their patch of sky two days in a row, unsure if that plane was searching for them. In the purple just before dusk they'd check their quarry, traps and snares in the forest, nets in the water—they'd check when they couldn't be spotted from the air. She wondered if the world really cared anymore about what they'd done in winter. She couldn't be sure.

Naked in the nearby lake or river under moonlight was a startling way to be, the water still chill in midspring. They gathered food, walked a black wood they felt their way through, paths they'd made and memorized, owls and bats sounding their way. They ate grayling, jackfish, bluebell shoots. Marten and fox and deer. Each night their eyes adjusted more to the dark. He could skin a deer by moon or fire. He knew which footfall was bear, which was moose. If ever they needed to be on paths in daylight he knew to stomp through the bush, hooting as he went, so as not to come suddenly upon a grizzly or brown bear. The scourge on this land, whatever curse had been here, fled when winter relented. The animals were back now after breakup.

She'd listen to him breathe, snore beside her. When his snores stopped she'd hold her own breath and try to hear the new morning outside through the sod walls. They'd sleep through the day and he'd wake her at the gloaming. After three days of hearing no planes they'd return once again to the daylight.

They relocated Bailey's grave once the ground was soft enough to pierce. They rescued him from the melting ice of the cemetery of Keelut and carried him in his plywood box deep into the taiga. Slone picked the spot beside the heather where they slept. He made her watch as he dug the hole, made her open the lid with a pry bar and look—not a glance but a look with two accepting eyes, and she did it because she knew that once she did, he'd never again mention what she'd done.

She possessed certain memories. She was a girl of five or six, summertime in the forest by the village, a forest of immense hemlock and oak. She could see rays of sun dispersed through the treetops, pollen suspended in the light like a galaxy of stars. Or those first years in the village schoolhouse, so long ago, their teacher a missionary from the States, a young man of beauty, she remembered. Dark hair and blue eyes—she was startled by the combination, had never seen it before. He had enough Bibles for all twelve children. He read verses as they sat rapt, not looking at their own text but at him, his lips, how they moved in such delight as if the words themselves were pleasure.

When she told Slone of her memories now, he said that memory is a trickster, the great deceiver. He couldn't recall half of what she could. They'd gone hand in hand everywhere together, surely he'd remember too if her memories had really happened, if the pollen in the shafts of sunlight had resembled stars that summer day, if the schoolteacher had given them Bibles. *He wants my memories too*, she thought. *He has my face and body, my every cell, and still he wants more, wants to steal my shadow too.*

As kids they'd come to this country for several days each summer with nothing but their bodies. She remembered they napped naked in the sun on beds of moss, on rocks of lichen, and later in the night they wrapped around each other for warmth. It was like that again now. Daily she grew round with another, with the new one he insisted on. Inside her she could hear already the sucking, sobbing, the pulse that led to a wailing for food, want of growth. And it was then she remembered she had other hopes.

At their spot in the valley they met their mother after breakup. She smacked him on the beard, held his chin firm in her hand, squeezed his lips. She told him, ordered him to make Medora pleased, and to make her pleased too. She said his teeth were filthy. He only nodded and looked away to the hills as Medora stifled a laugh.

In sunlight and moonlight both they walked far, and along the way she gathered salmonberries, bunchberries, mossberries, birch sap, and cottongrass stems. The fireweed she picked for its color. She could see it shine, really shine, in the first hour of daylight, and often she walked without him to collect the fireweed before they slept. The warm calm of the morning, these moments alone—she could not let them pass.

A late spring breeze came in through the entrance of their igloo and she woke with a knife in her hand, hovering above him as he slept. Their mother had given her a magazine a month earlier at their meeting place, and in it she'd read that dreams are useless. They mean nothing, hint at neither future nor past. They are the discard of the brain as the body slumbers. Why then, how did she see herself with the knife before she felt it in her hand, before she woke to find herself above him about to plunge a blade into his neck? Because, she knew, we call our wishes dreams, and she put down the knife to sleep again.

Acknowledgments

Feeling thanks to:

Bob Weil, torch in the night.

Steve Almond, rabbi, brother, friend.

John Stazinski, invaluable from inception.

Will Menaker, reader extraordinaire.

David Patterson, sapient 007.

The committed staff of W. W. Norton and Liveright, paragon in publishing.

Katie, Ethan, and Aiden, forgiving in this dark.

About the Author

William Giraldi *is the author of the novel* Busy Monsters *and fiction editor for the journal* AGNI *at Boston University. He lives in Boston with his wife and sons.*